Tracy Cogswell worked for hours digging in the cave with only one goal in mind—to bury himself alive!

He worked, zombielike, heedless of his growing horror, his pyramiding, mind-shattering terror. His mind screamed its agony, but he continued.

When it was done, he climbed into the coffin-like metal box and injected himself with a hypodermic filled with a combination of drugs he had concocted several days before. He leaned back, closed the metal top above him and—his true mind collapsing within itself—sighed and died.

But Tracy Cogswell awoke—he came alive again.

His first impression was: *I'm whole again. I'm in complete control of my own mind and body.*

Unconsciously, his hand, weak and trembling, went up to caress the scar which ran along the ridge of his jaw. The scar was gone! But it couldn't be—he'd had the scar since he was seventeen. And it came to him suddenly that his left arm was no longer stiff at the elbow. What happened?

And as the insane happenings came flooding back to him, Tracy realized that someone—or something—had taken over his body!

by Mack Reynolds:

AFTER UTOPIA

by
Mack Reynolds

WILDSIDE PRESS

Part One

REVOLUTION

Chapter One

Tracy Cogswell yawned again, gave up and left the letter in his typewriter unfinished. He could do it in the morning. It wasn't important anyway. Some instructions to a group of Montevideo.

He sometimes wondered at the advisability of the movement's making an effort in countries like Uruguay. What was the percentage? The decisions were going to be made in the most advanced countries: the United States, Common Europe, the Soviet Union, the People's Republic of China. The small nations could do no more than string along. The movement couldn't succeed in a country that wasn't highly industrialized and self-sufficient.

He was living in a small apartment, in a small apartment house, on Rue Dr. Fumey, Tangier, Morocco. In a city famed for the anonymity of its population, Tracy Cogswell was possibly the most anonymous of them all. At times he wondered if even Interpol was familiar with his efforts. They probably were. You didn't fight in Spain as a boy and twenty years later in Hungary —not to mention his other activities over the years

—without getting into the dossiers of the political police of the world, on both sides of the Curtain.

For a moment, he considered taking an amphetamine and knocking out some more work, but decided against it. That wasn't the way. Over a period of time you got more done without resorting to lifters, and Tracy Cogswell was trained in the long view.

He considered the pamphlet sitting on the coffee table next to his reading chair. It was an early work of the older Liebknecht, and Cogswell wasn't finding the going particularly easy, largely because he didn't know very much about what the situation in Imperial Germany had been before the turn of the century. However, in its way it was a classic, and Cogswell, though not a scholar by inclination, worked at acquiring a good foundation.

He decided that he was too groggy to concentrate on political economy, put his beret on his head, and left the room. Come to think of it, he hadn't been out all day and that didn't pay off. He'd wind up in a mental rut and there were too many people depending on his staying out of ruts. It was not by error that Tracy Cogswell was working full-time in the movement as a sort of international clearinghouse.

The apartment was a fifth floor walkup. During the three years that Cogswell had lived here, he'd had no visitors other than the plumber and, once, an electrician. And each time they'd appeared he'd gone to considerable trouble to alter the apartment's usual appearance, to make it look a bit less than what it really was. On the occasion where it was necessary to make explanations, Tracy put himself over as an unsuccessful writer, always at work on his serious novel. But the layout of his apartment was different from what even the most extensive researcher among writers might utilize. Too many files, too many stacks of mimeograph paper, too many pamphlets, leaflets, brochures; and his library was heavy with political economy, practically bare of anything else save a certain amount of history and reference.

Ordinarily, the recreation Cogswell allowed himself was rather limited to attending the local cinema. In the movies one can relax mentally and physically—and anonymously. Tonight, however, he had no desire for the Hollywood never-never land.

He walked down Rue Dr. Fumey to Rue De La Croix and turned right up to Mousa ben Nusair and the Bar Novara. This was the French section of town, and, except for an occasional haik clad, veiled fatima on her way home from a maid's job, you could have thought yourself in Southern France.

Paul Lund's bar had few claims to uniqueness so far as its appearance was concerned. It looked like any other bar.

The Vandyked owner-bartender was a typical resident of extradition-free Tangier. Exsmuggler, excon man, ex-half a dozen other types of criminal, the knowledge that Interpol was waiting for him anywhere out of Tangier kept him hemmed in; and kept him honest, for that matter. Paul Lund was smart enough not to foul his sole remaining nest.

Paul said, "Hi, Tracy. Haven't seen you for donkey's years."

Cogswell said, "I've been working. Having trouble

with my eighth chapter." He flicked his eyes over the two other occupants of the bar and recognized them both: an American sergeant of the marines, stationed at the local consulate, and a French teacher at the French lycée, a parlor-pink type who got his kicks out of supporting the Commie party line in public but who, in the finals, would probably turn out to be a rabid De-Gaulle man.

Paul was saying, "Eight chapters? Haven't you got any further than that with that poxy book of yours? Wot'll you have?"

"I'm rewriting," Cogswell said. "Let me have a pastis."

"Absinthe?"

"Hell no, that stuff fuzzes up my head for days."

Paul Lund poured an inch of Pernod into a tumbler and added three parts of cold water to it. Cogswell climbed up on one of the tiny bar's six stools and took a sip. He wondered how Desage was doing in Marseille. The police had nabbed him the week before, but they had nothing on him. France was one of the countries where the movement was legal; the authorities didn't like it, but it wasn't illegal. The same was true of the States and England. In the smaller countries they were underground. The smaller ones and the Soviet countries. It meant a bullet in the back of your head if you were caught behind the Curtain.

Paul winked at him and indicated the other two customers with a gesture of his head. "Jim and Pierre are solving all the troubles of the world."

Cogswell grunted. He listened uninterestedly to the

argument. It occurred to him that Jim looked surprisingly like a taller Mickey Rooney and Pierre Meunier like David Niven.

The argument wasn't unique. The American marine evidently got his opinions as well as his facts from *Time*. Pierre Meunier was reciting the Commie party line like a tape. In fact, as Cogswell listened he decided that Meunier wasn't even doing a particularly good job of that. He evidently wasn't aware of the fact that the party line had shifted in one or two particulars just that morning. Among other things, the American president was no longer a mad fascist dog; he was now a confused liberal. Meunier seemed to be of the opinion that he was still a mad fascist dog.

Jim finally turned to Tracy Cogswell plaintively. "Look, Mr. Cogswell, what do you think? Should the free world put up with the Russkies using the UN for a propaganda drum?"

"Free world!" Pierre Meunier snorted. "Yankee dollar imperialists on one extreme and feudalistic countries like Saudi Arabia on the other. The free world! Among others, Portugal, with its African slave colonies. Morocco, with its absolute monarchy. South Africa, that land of freedom! And Spain, that one! And the Dominican Republic, and Haiti, and Nicaragua, and Formosa, and South Korea and South Vietnam. All those freedom-loving countries."

Tracy Cogswell made a point of avoiding political discussions in Tangier. It wasn't his job to make individual converts. His position as an international coordinator remained possible so long as he remained anonymous. He also made a point of not arguing his political beliefs while he was drinking.

But in this case, something had happened. Jim had called him Mr. Cogswell. Unconsciously, Cogswell ran his right hand up over the scar that ran along the ridge of his jaw, disappearing into the sideburn. A mortar bomb fragment had creased him there at the debacle at Gerona during the Spanish civil war. The sideburn was now going gray. Jim must have been a child when the Abraham Lincoln Battalion had been all but wiped out at Gerona toward the end of the Spanish fracas.

Spain! That was where, even as a teenager, he'd gotten his bellyful of the damn Russians and where he'd begun to achieve some maturity in political economy. Spain, where the idealistic kids of a score of countries had flocked to fight for democracy and had wound up dying for Russian expediency.

Mr. Cogswell, yet! Was he that far along? Did he look like an old fogy to the marine?

He pushed his glass over toward Paul Lund and said, "Let's have another one."

To Jim he said, "Our position seems to be that the virtues of western democracy are so superior to the Soviet system that a few blasts on our trumpet will bring the Commie Jericho down. It might've been true, had the premise it rested upon been a little sounder. Unfortunately, the West doesn't form the community of unsullied virgins which the triumph of virtue predicates. As a matter of fact, the most shrill of the anti-Commie harridans are usually those of least political repute. For every Denmark or Holland, we've got a South Korea or Turkey. The big western powers seem to have recruited their allies not for their adherence to the principles we preach but for their opposition to the principles we oppose.''

Pierre Meunier was grinning happily. ''My point, exactly,'' he said.

Tracy Cogswell turned on him and snapped, ''As for the Commies, where did you get the idea that because one side might be wrong, the other must be right?''

Meunier said something like, ''Ung?''

Cogswell growled, ''I sometimes think that if there wasn't any such thing as the Communist party that it'd be to the interest of the western powers to create one. It makes the biggest bogy of all time. In the name of fighting the Commies you can pull just about anything in the way of keeping your people from examining your own institutions. In Guatemala, if the fruit pickers decide they need a union to get better pay than six bucks a week, the cry goes up *they're commies!* and the leaders are thrown into the jug. In South Africa the natives decide that some of the freedom they've been hearing about might be a good idea and start making some noises to that effect. Commies! the call goes up and they're slapped down flat. It applies to every country outside the Soviet ones. Any man in his right mind can see that what they've got in the Soviet Union is no answer, so even men of good will allow almost anything to be pulled just as long as its done in the name of fighting communism.''

Tracy Cogswell took an angry pull at his drink,

9

finishing it. "I think that the worst thing that ever happened to social progress was that damned premature Bolshevik revolution."

Paul Lund was laughing at him. "What side are you on, anyway?"

Cogswell slid off his stool and tossed two hundred francs to the counter. He grunted his disgust. "That was the point I was trying to make. It's about time the people in this world find out both sides are wrong and start looking for something else. Good night, gentlemen."

Jim said vacantly, "So long." He hadn't followed Cogswell's argument very well, but he could see by Meunier's unhappy expression that the party line hadn't been extolled.

Back in his apartment, he grunted sourly to himself. What did he think he was accomplishing? None of the three men he'd sounded off to were potential material for the movement. And there was a remote possibility that, as a result of his little curse-on-both-your-houses speech, word would get around that he, Tracy Cogswell, had rather strong political opinions, and that was the last thing he wanted.

He went out into his tiny kitchen and poured himself still another drink. Cogswell wasn't generally much for belting the bottle, but at the moment he felt the need for another drink. He brought his glass back to the living room and sat it on the coffee table next to his reading chair.

He picked up the Leibnecht pamphlet and thumbed through the pages idly. He was still in no mood for concentration.

Something alien flickered in his eyes, and he scowled and looked up at the wall opposite. There seemed to be some sort of light reflection. No, that wasn't the word.

Cogswell frowned, trying to figure out what it could be. Some reflection, or something, from somewhere. But where? Anything coming through the window that opened onto Rue Dr. Fumey would hardly . . .

He squinted at the vague flickering. What was it that it reminded him of? Why, a Fourth of July pinwheel, like they used to have when he was a kid in Cincinnati. One of the little penny ones.

His mind went back to Cincinnati.

The big swimming pool where the adults would throw in pennies and you'd dive for them. You could get enough to go to the movies if you worked at it long enough. Ten cents was the price of a kid's admission.

The movies in Cincinnati, back in the 1920s. He'd been a real fan. Lon Chaney, Hoot Gibson, Rin-Tin-Tin, Tom Mix, Our Gang.

The pinwheel was larger and turning faster. What in the world could it be? Quite an optical illusion. He knew that if he got up and walked over to it, either it would fade away or he would be able to determine what caused it. He felt too lazy to make the effort.

It still seemed to be growing in size.

That Pernod he'd had at Paul Lund's had hit him harder than he'd expected. Evidently he'd had too little dinner, and the alcohol had free range.

Of a sudden, Tracy Cogswell shook his head. He was getting drowsy and that wasn't right. That damned spinning was having hypnotic effect on him. He was going to have to . . .

Part of him backed away in astonishment. Why, he was actually, in a strange manner, under. Asleep, though still awake, from the effects of the spinning and . . . and something else. He didn't know what else. Good Jesus Christ, certainly Paul hadn't put something in his drink. No, that was ridiculous.

But now, in an impossible sort of way, part of his brain seemed to stand off and watch the rest of him. As though—what was the term the occult crackpots used?—as though his astral body was standing aloof from him and watching his every action.

Chapter Two

Tracy Cogswell stood up suddenly. The pinwheel was gone now. But there was still something there. And still his second self stood off and seemingly watched, completely puzzled. And there was even a touch of fear. Was he simply drunk?

Purposefully, Cogswell strode over to the heaviest of the steel files, fished his keys from his pocket and unlocked it. Inside the bottom drawer was a heavy strongbox. Another key opened it. He fished out more than a thousand dollars in pounds. French francs, fifty-dollar bills and British gold sovereigns. His emergency money. He also brought forth two bank-books, one on Barclay's in Gibraltar and one on the Moses Pariente bank here in Tangier, as well as his emergency forged Australian passport.

He tucked all of these into his pockets and went into the bedroom where he fished a suitcase from under the bed.

While his separate 'sane' self watched in growing amazement and disconcertedness, Tracy Cogswell rapidly packed his bag. He ignored the light Luger in the top drawer of his bureau and, contrary to his usual custom, packed no reading material at all.

Fifteen minutes after first seeing the pinwheel, he was carefully locking the door of his apartment behind him.

Down on the street, he strolled over to Rue Goya, tossing his apartment keys into a corner refuse can on the way. In front of the Goya Theatre, he hailed a Chico Cab and said, *"Je voudrais aller au Grand Zocco."*

This could only be a dream. A dream composed of too much work, too little relaxation, too much strain, and two of Paul Lund's heavy charges of Pernod.

But all the time he knew it was no dream.

In the Grand Zocco, the open-air market of the medina section of town, he paid the cab driver and started purposefully down the Rue Siaghines, which led to the Petit Zocco, once the most notorious square in the world.

Past him streamed the multiracial populace of what was possibly the most cosmopolitan city on earth. Berbers and Arabs, Rifs and Blue men, shabby Europeans from both sides of the Curtain. Indians in saris, Moslems in jellabas and shuffling babouche slippers. The Moorish fez, the Indian turban, the Jewish skullcap, the French beret. Rue Siaghines, the widest street in the medina, practically the only one in which you couldn't touch the walls along both sides while standing in the middle. Lined by Indian shops with the products of a hundred lands. Cameras from Germany, perfumes from France, watches from Switzerland.

And, for that matter, pornography from Japan, hashish from southern Morocco, heroin from Syria, aphrodisiacs from Egypt.

As he walked, his mentally clear astral self stood back in dumbfounded amazement. If this were no dream, then where was he going, what was he doing? Tracy Cogswell seldom came into the native section of Tangier. He had no reason to. His work and what little recreation he allowed himself all took place in the westernized section of town. He shopped in the French market, ate occasionally in a French or Spanish restaurant, visited the American library to read the papers and magazines, attended the cinema possibly two or three times a week.

He came to the Petit Zocco, crossed it, and took the narrow side street to the right, the one headed by what had been the Spanish post office when Tangier had been an International Zone. He ended at the Tannery Gate.

A hundred yards down it, he turned into Luigi's Pension, an establishment he'd never noticed before, one of a dozen similar cheap hotels.

Luigi, who Cogswell decided looked like a sinister version of the Mexican comedian Cantinflas, spoke English. Their business was quickly transacted. Tracy Cogswell's voice showed no indication of stress, certainly Luigi acted as though nothing untoward was going on. A man with a suitcase and an Australian passport was taking a room with full pension, three meals, at a cost of five hundred Moroccan francs per day. A bit over an American dollar.

15

The room was windowless, and drab beyond what the average westerner would expect. Tracy Cogswell didn't notice. He shoved the suitcase in a corner unopened, undressed himself, locked and bolted the door, and went to bed.

When the physical body fell off to sleep, the mental astral self, which was the sane Tracy Cogswell, lapsed into unconsciousness as well, unbelieving all the time. Tomorrow it would be different.

The next day it was not different.

Tracy Cogswell awoke, as did his mental otherself, the sane self. As purposefully as during the previous evening, he dressed, went down for his breakfast, and then out onto the street. He walked down the hill to the foot of the medina area, and then he went out through the old Tannery Gate and took a Chico Cab to the Moses Pariente bank. At the bank he withdrew all the money his account contained, more than eight thousand dollars. He took it in large bills and then set about other business.

He made reservations to fly over to Gibraltar. He sought out a real estate agent with whom he had never come in contact before, and, using his Australian name, started the preliminary steps toward buying a fairly large piece of land in the vicinity of Cape Spartel, out near the Grottos of Hercules.

His astral self stood back aghast. This was organization money. The movement raised its funds the hard way. There were few of even moderate means among the members. This money was the dollar bills, the fifty-cent pieces, the hundred-peseta notes, the five escudas, the twenty dinars, the ten piasters—bills and coins of dedicated believers in the movement all over the world. It was in his safekeeping to be used, here, there, wherever an emergency or an opportunity arose.

The buying of the land was only the beginning. His expenditures went on in shocking disregard of reason. He entered an electrical supply house and ordered equipment that he had never heard of; it was not available in Tangier, had to be brought down from Switzerland and Germany. He asked that it be flown!

Days went by. He had no idea what was motivating him, unless it was sheer insanity of a type he'd never heard of. He—his real self—had no control whatsoever over his actions. Nor any understanding of them.

He went to Gibraltar and secured the money he had on deposit there. Once again it was money that belonged to the movement.

He made arrangements with a local craftsman to build to peculiar specifications an airtight metal box some seven feet in length and resembling a coffin.

He made arrangements with a contractor to have a sturdy monument built on the piece of land he'd purchased near the Grottos.

He bought delicate tools, some of which had to be flown in from New York.

He had no idea of the passage of time. Weeks must have elapsed before he spotted Whiteley. Dan Whiteley, one of the movement's trouble-shooters, and Tracy Cogswell's oldest and best friend. They had been co-workers. Even in his peculiar mental condition, Tracy unconsciously stroked his stiff left elbow. The elbow had been shattered by a fluke shot from a machine pistol in the hands of one of Tito's bullyboys, that time when they'd smuggled Djilas across the Yugoslavian border. Dan Whiteley had been along on that operation. Easygoing in appearance, resembling Jimmy Stewart of twenty years earlier, he was a good man in the clutch.

There was no doubt about the tall, rangy Canadian's reason for being in Tangier. No doubt at all. When last Cogswell had heard from him, he'd been on an assignment in the Argentine.

His sane self, his inner self, wanted to dash forward and throw himself into his friend's hands. Anything was better than this, even death. His stolen body was betraying everything he had stood for during his adult life. Already, he had practically disposed of the full amount of money entrusted to him by the Executive Committee.

But he didn't dash forward to greet Whiteley. Instead, he shrank back into an alcove and watched the other man narrowly. The Canadian hadn't spotted him. Tracy Cogswell followed along behind, the quarry stalking the hunter.

They left the medina, proceeded up the Rue de la Liberte to the Place de France and then down ultramodern Boulevard Pasteur to Rue Goya, and then over to Moussa ben Maussair. It was obvious where Whiteley was going now. Tracy Cogswell held back more than a full block and watched the other disappear into Paul Lund's bar. He didn't know how long Dan

Whiteley had been in town, but obviously the other was hot on his trail.

He returned to his pension room, dragged out some of his newly arrived packages, a soldering iron and other new tools, and set to work.

To work on what? He had no idea. Most of the tools were strange to him, as was the other equipment he had ordered. Tracy Cogswell had never been mechanically inclined, but everything he hid now belied that fact. He worked almost until dawn.

Now that Whiteley was in town, Cogswell stayed off the streets as much as possible. He transacted as much business over the phone as he could.

For some things he had to emerge. The time, for instance, that he rented the truck, had his metal cabinet hoisted aboard, and transported it out to the monument on his Cape Spartel land. The monument, also completed by now, reminded his inner self of one of the Moslem holy men's mausoleums that abounded in northern Morocco.

Somehow, despite his stiff elbow, he managed to manhandle the heavy cabinet from the truck and into the small inner chamber of the monument. Why he did this, he had no idea whatsoever.

He was evidently waiting for something. He knew not what. He stuck to his room, emerging only to take his meals. Even that he discontinued after spotting Whiteley passing the pension's street window one day. From then on, he had Luigi deliver his food to his room. The little Italian said nothing. Probably he had seen men on the run before and was possibly wondering if it was the sort of thing where he might pick up a few thousand francs by informing on his guest.

A piece of delicate electrical equipment from Sweden finally came. He dumped all of his clothes and other belongings from his suitcase and filled it with some of his precision tools, the equipment he had been working on, and a small folding entrenching tool.

He carried his suitcase out of his room, locking the door behind him, paid off Luigi, and made his way into the street. As he walked down from the Petit Zocco toward the harbor and the Avenue de Espana, where he could get a cab, he heard the sound of quick pattering feet behind him.

He spun and stared. It was Dan Whiteley, running hard.

Tracy Cogswell sprinted down the long incline and past the Grand Mosque. He caromed from time to time against protesting Moors and Arabs. Behind him, the lanky Dan Whiteley was shouting in rage.

He was comparatively safe. Even if Whiteley had gunfire in mind, it couldn't be done here. Besides, a dead Tracy Cogswell could never return the nearly twenty thousand dollars he'd had custody of, and Whiteley had no way of knowing it had all been spent by now. Besides, again, no matter how dedicated the Canadian might be, Cogswell doubted that the other could find it within him to shoot his old companion. They'd been through too much together.

He slammed out onto the Avenue de Espana and with

providential luck, ran immediately into a Chico Cab the moment he emerged from the Marine Gate. He climbed in, yelled at the driver to take him to the Boulevard Pasteur. He peered over his shoulder, saw the frantic Dan Whiteley trying to find a cab and failing.

On Pasteur Boulevard he exchanged cabs and rode up the Rue Alexandria to the Marshan district in the vicinity of the Carthaginian tombs. Here he switched cabs again and ordered the driver to the Grottos of Hercules on the Atlantic coast.

It was dark by the time they arrived. He dismissed the driver, who looked at him strangely for only a brief moment and then took off. Tracy Cogswell had given him, in way of a tip, the last francs he had in his pockets.

For a moment, Tracy Cogswell stared out over the sea, watching the beer-head waves break in their desperation against the volcanic rock that lined the shore at this point. Some of the grottos could be seen here. He could see the Grottos of Hercules, where the mythological Greek hero had supposedly lived while throwing up the Pillars of Hercules and seeking the Golden Apples of the Hesperides. Probably the world's strongest man had never existed, but Neolithic remains in the grottos indicated that humans had been here long before the Greeks had infiltrated the peninsula that now bears their name.

He took up his suitcase and walked the mile or so to the monument he had constructed. He entered it and bolted the heavy door behind him.

His conscious mind was beginning to find a horror that surpassed anything he had suffered thus far. He realized that the culmination of all that had gone on for these past weeks was now upon him. And he still had no conception of what he was about.

Tracy Cogswell brought the entrenching tool from his bag, unfolded it, and began to dig. In about two hours he had broken through to a chamber beneath: a natural chamber, related to the larger grottos in the vicinity.

He tugged and levered his large metal box until he was finally able to lower it into the small cave. He set up a heavy flashlight, brought forth his tools and began attaching the equipment he'd labored upon so long to the various entries and nipples that had obviously been built to receive it. He worked for many hours.

Finally, it was through. Somehow he knew it was through.

With the entrenching tool, he then began steps to close the cave's narrow entrance behind him. *To bury himself alive!*

He strained mentally, his mind screaming its agony, without effect. He worked, zombielike, heedless of his growing horror, his pyramiding, mind-shattering horror.

When it was done, he climbed into the metal box. And now he understood. The container which looked like a coffin was exactly that.

He brought a hypodermic needle from a set that he had purchased a week before, filled it with a combination of drugs he had concocted several days before, and pressed it home in his left arm.

He leaned back, closed the metal top above him, flicked the lugs securely and—his true mind collapsing within itself—sighed and died.

Chapter Three

Tracy Cogswell awoke. That isn't quite the word. He came alive again.

His first impression was: I'm whole again. I'm in complete control of my own mind and body.

Unconsciously, his hand, weak and trembling, went up to caress the scar which ran along the ridge of his jaw. The scar was gone. But it couldn't be, he'd had the scar since the age of seventeen.

And it came to him suddenly that his left arm was no longer stiff at the elbow. Was this his own body? What had happened?

Everything was flowing back to him. The insane happenings. His body taken over by . . . by whatever it was that had taken it over. The monument, the coffin, the expenditure of all the money the International Executive Committee had entrusted him with.

He looked about the room. A man of approximately thirty years of age was seated beside the bed, evidently waiting for Tracy to awaken. He was slight of build and looked considerably like the younger Leslie Howard playing some easygoing part. He seemed to be interested in a piece of what looked like green stone. He was holding it in a somewhat cramped fashion, running his thumb over its surface.

His eyes came idly to Tracy Cogswell's face and lit up when he noticed Cogswell was awake. He had a lazy charm which was immediately felt.

He said, "Well, awake at last, eh?"

Cogswell took in the other's clothes, or, rather, the lack of them. A brief vest-like top garment beneath which the chest was bare, a kilt of some ultrasoft material, and sandals. He'd never seen such garb anywhere. He still looked like Leslie Howard, but as though the actor was done up for a masquerade.

The other came to his feet in a fluid, lazy motion. "My name's Edmonds," he said. "Jo Edmonds. Just a moment, I'll be right back."

He left, and Tracy Cogswell looked about the room. His mind felt blank. There was too much to assimilate. The room was attractive enough, comfortable looking, but as alien in appearance as the costume of . . . what was the fellow's name? . . . Jo Edmonds.

Edmonds returned with an older man, who was obviously excited.

"Well," he said happily. "Well, we did it, didn't we?"

"What?" Cogswell said, his voice still stiff.

The older man's costume was as bizarre as Edmonds' as bizarre but without similarity. His clothing resembled the haiks worn by the Arab women, or, better still, a Roman toga: white and draping.

Jo Edmonds said, "Tracy Cogswell, may I introduce Academician Walter Stein." He paused for a moment, smiled lazily, and added, "the genius responsible for your presence here." His thumb was still caressing the bit of green stone.

Cogswell felt too weak even to come to his elbow. "Why?" he said.

Stein bustled over to him, patted his pillow, obviously pleased. "Now, no more now," he chortled. "Later, when you're stronger. Now you must rest. First, we'll get just a touch of food into you, and then you'll rest. Oh, there must be quite a bit of rest at first."

That was all right. Almost anything was all right. Food and rest. That was obviously the ticket. All problems could be solved later.

The food came, brought by a girl in her late twenties who looked somewhat like Paulette Goddard back when that actress had been the reigning beauty of Hollywood. She also had some facial resemblance to the older of the two men.

The food consisted of a thick soup. She watched him, wide-eyed and speechless, as she fed him. She wore an outfit composed of a bikini-type top, a pair of peddle-pushers, and startling shoes of golden color.

Yes, Paulette Goddard, Tracy thought. She looks something like Paulette Goddard, and she has a better figure. Wherever I am, they've got some strange ideas about clothes.

When he awoken the second time, there was more food. After a while, they'd gotten him up into a chair and pushed him out onto a terrace. He recognized the scene. No other houses were in sight, but there was no doubt about it, he was within a mile of Cape Spartel, atop the mountain which rises above Tangier and looks out over Spain and the Atlantic. Over in that direction was Trafalgar. When Nelson had fought his last naval battle with the fleets of Bonaparte, residents had been able to hear the thunder of the guns.

There was little else he could indentify. The architecture of the house was extreme to the point of making Frank Lloyd Wright's wildest conceptions a primitive adobe by comparison. The chair in which he sat was wheelless, but it carried him at the gentlest direction of Jo Edmonds' hand.

The three of them—the girl's name, it turned out, was Betty Stein—accompanied him to the terrace, treating him as though he were porcelain. Tracy Cogswell was still weak, but he was alert enough now to be impatient and curious.

He said, "My elbow."

Academician Stein fluttered over him. "Don't overdo, Tracy Cogswell, don't overdo."

Jo Edmonds grinned, and, turning on his charm, said, "We had your elbow and various other, ah, deficiencies taken care of before we woke you."

Tracy was about to say "Where am I?" but he knew where he was. Something strange was going on but he knew where he was. He was within a few miles of Tangier proper and in the strangest house he'd ever seen, and certainly the most luxurious. For a moment that fact struck him. He was, on the face of it, in the hands of the opposition. Only a multimillionaire could

27

afford this sort of an establishment, and none of the ultrawealthy were sympathetic to the movement.

He considered Jo Edmonds' words and accepted them. But he realized the implications of accepting them. He'd had that arm worked on in London by a man who was an organization sympathizer and possibly the world's outstanding practitioner in the field. He had saved the elbow, but let Tracy know it would never be strong again. Now it was strong.

By the third day, he was up and around and beginning to consider his position and how to escape from it. He kept his mind from some of the more far-out aspects of the thing. Explanations would come later. For now, he wanted to evaluate his situation.

He didn't seem to be a prisoner, but that was beside the point. You didn't have to have steel bars to be under duress. The three oddly garbed characters who had him here seemed to be of good will, but Tracy Cogswell was experienced enough in world political movements to know that the same man who sentenced you to the gas chamber or firing squad could be a gentle soul who loved his children and spent his spare time puttering happily in a rock garden.

There were a few moderately wealthy persons in the movement but certainly no one this wealthy. He was in the hands of the enemy, and, considering the amount of trouble they had gone to, there was something big in the wind.

He wondered about the possibilities of escape. No, not yet. For one thing, he'd never make it. He was still too weak, particularly if he had to fight his way out. For another thing, he had to find out what was happening. He had to ferret out information about what was going on. Perhaps . . . just perhaps . . . there was some explanation that would make sense to Dan Whiteley and the International Executive Committee. At least that was the straw he clung to.

He had made his own way out to the terrace again and had seated himself on a piece of furniture somewhat similar to a lawn chair. That was one of the things that got to him. Even the furniture in this ultra-automated house was so far out as to be unbelievable.

Jo Edmonds drifted easily onto the terrace and raised his eyebrows at Cogswell. He was wearing shorts today, and slippers that seemed somehow to cling to the bottom of his feet, although there wasn't a strap on top. He was flipping, as though it was a coin, the flat green stone.

"How do you feel?" he said.

Cogswell said irritably, indicating the stone, "What in the hell's that?"

Edmonds said, in his mild voice, "This? A piece of imperial jade. Do you enjoy tactile sensation?"

Cogswell scowled at him. "What in the devil are you talking about?"

Edmonds said, and there was enthusiasm in his usually lazy voice, "The Chinese have been familiar with the quality of jadeite—a sodium aluminum silicate, belonging to the pyroxenes, you know—for centuries. They've developed its appreciation into an advanced art form. I have a small collection and make a point of spending an hour or so every day over it. It takes

29

considerable development to obtain the sensual gratification possible by stroking jade. Some people never develop it.''

Cogswell said disgustedly, ''You mean to say you've got nothing better to do with your time than to pet a piece of green stone?''

Edmonds was somewhat amused. ''There are less kindly things to which to devote yourself,'' he said.

Walter Stein emerged from the house and looked worriedly at Cogswell. He said, ''How are you feeling? You're not overexerting yourself, are you?''

A Paul Lucas type, Tracy had already decided. Paul Lucas playing the part of an M.D.

Tracy said, ''I'm all right, but, look, I've gotten to the point where if I don't find out what's going on, I'll go completely around the corner. Let's get to some explanations. I realize that somehow or other you rescued me from a crazy nightmare I got myself into. My only explanation is that I must have had a complete nervous breakdown. I didn't think I was the type.''

Jo Edmonds chuckled, good-naturedly.

Cogswell turned on him. ''What's so damn funny?''

Academician Stein held up a hand. ''I'm afraid, Mr. Cogswell, that Jo's humor is poorly taken. You see, we didn't rescue you from yourself. No, hardly. It was we who put you into your predicament. Please forgive us, but it was for a very good reason.''

Cogswell stared at him.

Stein said uncomfortably, almost sheepishly. ''Do you know where you are Tracy Cogswell?''

''Yes, I know where I am. Tangier is a few miles

30

over in that direction. And that's Spain, over the water there.''

Walter Stein said, ''That's not exactly what I meant. Let's cut corners, Mr. Cogswell. You are now in the year 2045 A.D., or at least you would be if we still used the somewhat inefficient calendar of your era. We haven't been utilizing it since the turn of the century. We now call this the year 45 New Calendar.''

Cogswell thought to himself that it didn't really come as too much of a surprise. He knew that it was going to be something like that.

''Time travel,'' he said aloud. It was a field of thought he had never investigated, but he was dimly aware of the conception. He had seen a movie or two, such as *Berkley Square,* in which Tyrone Power had played a time traveler who found himself in the world of Boswell and Dr. Johnson, and he had read a few short stories over the years. And hadn't he read a short novel by H.G. Wells or somebody about a time machine that took the inventor far into the future?

''Well, not exactly,'' Stein said, scowling a bit. ''But, yes, in a way.''

Edmonds laughed softly. ''You're not being very definite, Walter.''

The older man had taken a seat on the low stone parapet that surrounded the terrace. Now he leaned forward, elbows on knees, and clasped his hands together. His voice was less than comfortable. He said, ''Time travel isn't possible, Mr. Cogswell, not so far as we know. The paradoxes would seem to be insurmountable.''

31

"But you just said——"

The other was obviously seeking for words that would make sense. He said, "What it amounts to is that you've been in a state of suspended animation, I suppose you could call it."

For Tracy Cogswell things were beginning to fit into place. There were still a lot of loose ends, but the tangle was coming out.

He said slowly, working it out as he went. "But you would have had to travel back to my day to hypnotize me. To take over my actions."

Stein said, his tone very serious, "Not our physical selves, Tracy Cogswell. It is impossible to send matter through time. Except forward, of course, at the usual pace. However, the mind can and does travel in time. Memory is nothing more than that. In dreams, the mind even travels ahead sometimes, although we do not as yet understand how that is possible, and it is usually in such a haphazard manner that it is impossible to measure, to get into a laboratory for study and to gather usable data."

Jo Edmonds said, "In your case, it was a matter of going back into the past, seizing control of your mind and then your body, and forcing you to perform yourself the steps that would lead to your, ah, suspended animation, as the academician puts it."

For some reason, the younger man's easygoing tone irritated Cogswell. "What in the hell's an academician?"

Edmonds raised his eyebrows. "Oh," he said, "that's right. The degree evolved after your period. It was found that even the Ph.D. had become somewhat commonplace, so the higher one of academician was created. It is quite difficult to attain.''

Cogswell's irritation was growing. The two of them, no matter how well intentioned they might seem to be now, had a lot to answer for. Besides that, they were so comfortably clean, so obviously well fed, so unworried and adjusted. They had it made. It probably took a dozen servants to keep up this house, to wait hand and foot on Betty and Walter Stein and Jo Edmonds, to devote their lives to these two so that they could continue to look so comfortably sleek. And how many people did it take, slaving away somewhere in industry or office, to provide the funds necessary to maintain this fabulous establishment? Parasites!

Tracy said flatly, ''So you figured out a way of sending back through time. Of hypnotizing me. Of providing my hypnotized body with information that allowed it to put itself into a state of suspended animation. To accomplish this, I absconded with some twenty thousand dollars. Perhaps that isn't a great deal in your eyes, but it was composed of thousands upon thousands of tiny donations . . . donations to a great cause. An attempt to make the world a better place to live in. To end poverty and war.''

Stein was frowning worriedly and clucking under his breath. But the ever easygoing Edmonds had an amused expression on his face, as though Cogswell couldn't have said anything further out.

Cogswell snapped, ''When I've got back some of my strength, I'd like to take a crack at wiping some of that vacant-minded amusement off your pretty face, Ed-monds.''

''Sorry, old chap,'' Edmonds said. ''No idea of irritating you was intentioned.''

Tracy snarled, ''For now I'd like to know this: Why!''

The girl, Betty, came out then and looked from one to the other. She said impatiently, as though the others were idiots, ''What are you doing, Father? And you, Jo? Good heavens, look at the state Mr. Cogswell is in. I thought you weren't going to discuss this project with him until he was suitably recovered.''

This project, yet! What project! Tracy Cogswell was getting more out of his depth by the minute.

He glared at the girl. ''I want to know what the big idea is!'' he snapped. ''I've been kidnápped. On top of that, in spite of the fact that seemingly I did it, actually you bastards are guilty of stealing twenty thousand dollars of money that was intrusted with me. I want an explanation.'' He could feel the flush of extreme rage mounting over his face, and he didn't give a good goddamn.

''See?'' she said indignantly to Academician Stein and Jo Edmonds. You've upset him terribly.''

The two men looked at Cogswell in embarrassment. ''Sorry. You're right,'' Edmonds said to her. He turned on his heel and left, nervously thumbing his piece of jade.

Stein began bustling and clucking again, attempting to take Cogswell's pulse.

Tracy jerked his arm away. ''Damn it,'' he said,

34

ignoring the girl. "I want to know what this is all about. You bastards have a lot to answer for."

"Later, later," the older man soothed.

"Later, my ass!"

It was Betty who said, "See here . . . Tracy. You're among friends. Let us do it our way. Answers will come soon enough." She added, like a nurse to a child, "Tomorrow, perhaps, I'll take you for a pleasant ride over Gibraltar and up the Costa del Sol."

In the morning, for the first time, Tracy Cogswell ate with the rest of them in a small breakfast room. The more he saw of the house, the more he was impressed by its efficient luxury. Impressed wasn't quite the word. Cogswell had never known this sort of life, and he had never desired to. The movement had been his life. Food, clothing, and shelter were secondary things, necessary only to keep him going. The luxuries? Oh, he liked good food when it came to him . . . and good drink, for that matter. But he had seen little of them, and he wasn't particularly regretful.

He'd expected to be waited upon by Moorish servants, or possibly even French or Spanish ones. However, evidently he was being kept under wraps. The table in the breakfast nook was automated; it operated by dials. Betty did the ordering, and when the dishes appeared—the table top had sunk and then returned with them—served them.

The food, admittedly, was out of this world. He wondered if Betty Stein had cooked it herself, earlier. But no, of course not. Betty Stein was much too decorative to have any useful qualities. She was dressed today

35

in a brief outfit that looked something like Tarzan's wife, Jane, used to wear in Edgar Rice Burroughs movies.

The conversation was desultory, and obviously deliberately so. Walter Stein even avoided Tracy's eyes for some reason. However, there was still amusement behind those of Jo Edmonds.

Toward the end of the meal, Stein said, "How do you feel, Mr. Cogswell? Up to the little jaunt that Betty suggested yesterday? You're sure it wouldn't tire you too much? After all, it's been just a few days."

Tracy growled, "I don't see why not."

The way he felt, the more information he gathered about his surroundings, the better prepared he would be to take care of himself when and if he went on the run from whatever situation they'd gotten him into. In his time, Tracy Cogswell had been on the run more than once; his experience had taught him to case the area as well as he could.

He was able to walk by himself to the garage, although Academician Stein bumbled worriedly along beside him all of the way.

Cogswell was settled into the front seat of a vehicle that didn't look so much different from a sport sedan of his own time, except for the fact that it lacked wheels. Betty took her place behind the controls, beaming at him reassuringly. The controls didn't look too much different from those of a car of the late 1950s, a steering wheel, some foot pedals, and a conglomeration of gadgets on the dashboard.

The difference came, Cogswell found, when they

emerged from the garage, proceeded a few feet, and then took to the air, without wings, rotars, propeller, jets, or any other noticeable method of support or propulsion.

She could see he was taken aback and said, "What's the matter, Tracy?"

Cogswell said wryly, "I hadn't expected this much progress in this much time."

"Oh, you mean the car?"

So they still called them cars.

"You needed wings in my day," Cogswell said dryly.

She was obviously a skilled driver . . . or pilot, as the case might be.

"I sometimes get my dates mixed," Betty said, making a small moue. "But I thought that you were beginning to get air-cushioned cars, hover-craft, that sort of thing, in your time. And hadn't Norman Dean already begun his work?"

"Never heard of him," he said. Cogswell was looking down at the countryside beneath him.

Tangier had changed considerably. It had obviously become an ultrawealthy resort area. Gone was the Casbah, with its Moorish slums going back a thousand years and more. Gone was the medina with its teeming thousands of poverty-stricken Arabs and Riffs.

Tracy grunted to himself. He supposed that as Europe's and America's wealthy had discovered the climactic and scenic advantages of northern Morocco, they had displaced the multitude of natives who had formerly made uncomfortable by their obvious need those few of the well-to-do who had lived here before. The rich hate to see the poor; it makes them uncomfortable. Tracy Cogswell remembered the old story about the lush in the nightclub listening tearfully to a plaintive blues singer and saying, "Throw her out, she's breaking my heart."

There were quite a few of the flying cars such as he and Betty were in. That was a good thing, though. With flight on various levels, there was no congestion. However, he assumed that probably other traffic problems had evolved.

Betty put on speed and in a matter of five or ten minutes they were circling Gibraltar, perhaps the world's most spectacular landfall. Here too the signs of the military of his own period had given way to villas and what he assumed were luxury apartment buildings.

Tracy said, "Where are all the stores, garages, and other business establishments?"

She said, "Underground."

"Where you can't see them and be bothered by their unattractiveness, eh?"

"That's right," she told him, evidently missing his sarcastic note.

They flew north along the coast, passing Estapona, Marbella and Fuengirola. Cogswell was impressed. Even in his own time the area had been booming, but he had never expected to see anything like this. Why, the whole coast seemed dotted with villas.

"It's much too crowded," Betty said in disgust. "I've always been amazed that so many people gravitate to the warm climates."

38

He said impatiently, "Everyone would, wouldn't they, given the wherewithal?"

"But why? She was surprised at his words. "Why not stay in areas where you have season changes? For that matter, why not spend some seasons in the far north and enjoy the extremes of snow and cold weather? Comfortable homes can be built in any climate."

Cogswell grunted. "You sound like that queen —what was her name?—who said 'Let them eat cake.' "

Betty frowned not getting it. "Marie Antoinette? How do you mean I sound like her?"

Tracy Cogswell said impatiently, "Look. You people with lots of dough don't realize what it can mean for somebody without it to spend some time in the sun. And . . . if possible, and it usually isn't . . . to finally retire in a desirable climate in your old age. It's something a lot of poor working stiffs dream of, but you wouldn't know about that."

Betty looked at him from the side of her eyes and frowned. "Dough?" she said.

"Money," Cogswell said, still impatient. "Sure, if you have piles of money, you can build swell houses even up in Alaska, and live comfortably. You can live comfortably just about anywhere, given piles of money. But for most people, who've probably lived the greater part of their lives in some near-slum, in some stinking city, the height of ambition is to get into a warm climate and have a little bungalow in which to finish off the final years."

Suddenly, Betty laughed.

Tracy Cogswell froze up, his face went expression-less. Until this, he had rather liked the beautiful girl. Now she was showing the typical arrogance of the rich.

She indicated the swank villas beneath them. They were flying over Torremolinos now, which had once been an art colony. She said, "Were you under the impression, Tracy, that those people down there had lots of money?"

That took time to sink in. It couldn't possibly mean what he first thought.

Tracy said, "Possibly they don't have by your standards, but by mine, yes."

Betty said flatly, "None of them have any money at all, and neither do I."

That was too much. He gaped at her.

Betty said, "There is no such thing as money any more, and there hasn't been for quite a while. It was eliminated decades ago."

He figured that he understood now, and said, "Well, it's the same thing. Whatever the means of exchange is, credit cards, or whatever."

Betty laughed again and there was honest amusement in her voice, not condescension. She said, and her voice was gentle now, "Tracy Cogswell, in all those years you belonged to your movement, in all the years of dedication, did you really think, really inwardly believe in your heart of hearts, that someday it might come true? That someday the millineum would arrive, Utopia be achieved?"

A deep cold went through him. He closed his mouth but continued to stare in disbelief at her.

"Tracy," she said gently, "your movement was successful more than sixty years ago."

After a long moment, he said, "Look, could we go back to the house? I could use a drink."

She laughed still once again and spun the wheel of the hover-craft.

Chapter Four

They were all three amused by his reactions, but it was a friendly amusement and with a somehow wry connotation which Tracy Cogswell didn't quite get. So many things were bubbling through his head, so many questions to ask, he didn't even have time for a complete answer before he was hurrying on to the next one.

"And the Russkies? What happened over there?" he demanded. "The Soviet Union and the other Commie countries?"

Jo Edmonds said, "The same as everywhere else. Overnight, the contradiction that had built up through the decades of misrule and misdirection finally boiled over. It was one of the few places where there was much violence. The Communists had gone too far, had done too much to too many, to have been allowed peaceful retirement."

Betty shook her head. "According to accounts of the period, in some places it was quite horrible."

Tracy Cogswell drew from his own memories pictures of members of the secret police hanging by their heels from lamp posts. He had been active with the Freedom Fighters in Budapest, during the 1956 uprising against the Russians. "Yes," he said uncomfortably. Then he asked, "But countries like India, the African nations, South America and the other undeveloped countries. How do they stand now?"

Academician Stein was chuckling softly. "These things seem so long ago to us," he said. "It's almost unbelievable that they can be news to an intelligent adult. The backward countries? Why, given the all-out support of the most industrially advanced, they were brought up to a common level within a decade or two."

"It was a universally popular effort," Betty added. "Everybody pitched in. Instead of sending so-called aid to those countries, consisting largely of military equipment, we sent real aid and no strings attached."

"Yes, yes, of course," Cogswell blurted. "But, look . . . look, the population explosion. What happened there?"

Jo Edmonds, who was sitting relaxed in an armchair near the fireplace of the living room, a drink in one hand, his inevitable piece of jade in the other, said easily, "Not really much of a problem, given world government and universal education on a high level. If you'll remember, the large families were almost always to be found in the most backward countries, or among the most backward elements in the advanced countries. Education and really efficient methods of birth control ended the problem. Population is static now, if not declining. It was the European countries and Japan that first turned the corner. In the year 1972, West Germany

43

lost population, the first of the advanced countries to do so.''

''Look,'' Cogswell said happily, ''could I have another drink? This must be the damnedest thing that ever happened to a man. Why, why it's as though Saint Paul woke up in the year, well, say, 1400 A.D. and saw the strength of the church·that he had founded. He would have flipped, just as I'm doing.''

All three of them laughed at him again and Jo Edmonds got up, slipped his jade into a side pocket and went over to the sideboard and mixed him another drink.

Tracy Cogswell said, ''That reminds me of something. How about servants? It must take a multitude of maids to run a house like this.''

Betty made a moue at him. ''Nonsense. You aren't very good at extrapolation, are you, Tracy? Why, even in your own day in the advanced countries the house was automated to the point where even the well-to-do didn't have domestic help. Today, drudgery has been eliminated. Anyone can have just about as large a house as they want and keep it up by devoting only a few moments a day to its direction.''

It was still all but inconceivable to him. ''And everybody, just everybody can afford a place like this?''

It was the academician's turn again. As they'd all been doing, he prefaced his explanation with a laugh. ''Given automation and cheap, all but free power, and what is the answer? Ultraabundance for everyone. Surely the signs must have been present in your day. That was the goal of your organization, was it not?''

"Yes," Cogswell said, shaking his head. "Yes, of course." Then he added, his voice very low, "Jesus H. Christ."

They all laughed with him.

Jo Edmonds brought the fresh drink and Cogswell knocked it back in one long swallow.

He considered for a moment. "Look," he said, "I don't suppose anyone remembers what happened to a fellow named Dan Whiteley."

"Whiteley?" the Academician scowled.

"He was a member of the organization," Tracy explained. "A very active one."

"Dan Whiteley," Betty said. "I read something about him. Let me see. He was a Canadian."

"That's right," Tracy Cogswell said, leaning forward. "He was from Winnipeg."

"Did you know him?" Betty said, her voice strange.

He said slowly, "Yes, yes I knew him quite well." Unconsciously, he stroked his left elbow. The others had been in favor of leaving him behind. Dan had carried him, one way or the other, half the night. Toward morning, Tito's secret police had brought up dogs and they'd been able to hear them baying only half a mile or so behind.

Betty said gently, "The Communists got him when he was trying to contact some of their intellectuals and get your movement going in China. He succeeded, but later was caught and shot in, I believe, Hankow. He's now sort of a martyr. Students of the period know about him."

Cogswell took a deep breath. "Yeah," he said.

"That's the way Dan Whiteley would have ended. In action. Could I have another drink?"

Stein said, "You're not overdoing, are you?"

"No, of course not. Look, how about cancer, and space flight, and how about interracial problems and juvenile delinquency?"

"Hold it!" Jo Edmonds told him. Somehow there was a strained quality in the laugh that Cogswell couldn't quite put his finger on.

Stein said, "You can imagine how long any of the old diseases lasted once we began to devote the amount of time to them that our scientists had formerly put into devising methods of destroying man."

Betty said, "About the space program. We have a few observatories and some laboratories on the moon, and orbiting communications satellites."

Edmonds brought the drink and Tracy took a long swallow and then shook his head.

Walter Stein was quickly on his feet. "See here," he said, "you're pale. We've allowed you to push yourself too far." He clucked unhappily. "Betty was premature, this morning. We hadn't expected to allow you so much excitement for several days yet. Now, back to bed for you. We can talk further, in the morning."

Tracy nodded. "I feel a little tired and a little tight," he admitted.

He went back to the room they had assigned him and undressed, his mind still in a whirl. In bed, just before dropping off into sleep, he gazed up at the ceiling. What did he feel like? He felt something like he had as a

46

kid, back there in Cincinnati, when tomorrow was going to be Christmas, when tomorrow was going to be the best day that ever was.

He was drifting off into sleep before a worrying thought wriggled up from below. He never quite grasped it all. He remembered once when his father had been unemployed and Christmas had been bleak. He never quite grasped it all. However, his subconscious worked away.

They were waiting for him on the terrace, which they had set up for breakfast, when he emerged in the morning. He was dressed, as they were, in most imaginative clothes. Cogswell had already come to the conclusion that fashions and styles were a thing of yesteryear; people dressed in the most comfortable way they damn well pleased. He supposed that followed; fashion had largely been a matter of sales promotion, and he assumed that sales promotion was in the doldrums these days. His own Bermuda shorts, sports shirt and sandals had been beside his bed when he had awakened.

And for the first time since his being brought out of hibernation, or whatever you could call it, he felt really fit, both mentally and physically alert. He felt that he was ready for anything.

After they'd exchanged the standard good mornings and questioned him on his well being, Tracy came immediately to the point.

"See here," he told them. "Yesterday, I was pretty well taken up with enthusiasm. I doubt if many men live to see their own ideas of Utopia achieved. In fact, looking back, I can't think of a single example. But, anyway, now I'd like to get some basic matters cleared up. I'd like to get down to the nitty-gritty."

Jo Edmonds finished his cup of coffee, leaned back in his chair, fished his piece of jade from a pocket, and began fiddling with it. He said, "Fire away, old chap," but he, like the other two, seemed to have a faint element of tension.

Cogswell took his chair and said, "All right now. As I understand it, through a method devised by the academician, here, you were able to send his mind back in time to my age, hypnotize me, or whatever you want to call it, and force me to take the steps that resulted in my being, well, deep-frozen."

Walter Stein shrugged. He still reminded Cogswell of Paul Lucas playing the part of an anxious scientist. "That's a sufficient explanation," he said. "At least as near as I would expect a layman to get."

Cogswell looked at him questioningly. "What was all that jazz about the monument, and that cave or grotto or whatever it was beneath it?"

Stein said, "We had to have some place to leave your body where it wouldn't be discovered for a period of nearly a century. A cave beneath a holy man's tomb was as good a bet as any. Even today, such monuments are respected by the local people."

"I see," Cogswell said, pouring some coffee into his cup. "I've got some mind-twisting questions I want to ask about what seem to me some really far out paradoxes, but they can wait. First, what happened

48

after I'd gone? What do the records say about my disappearance? What did the International Executive Committee do? What kind of a report was given out about me to the membership of the movement?" As he spoke, his face tightened.

Betty took up the ball. She said, very softly, "Remember, Tracy, when I told you yesterday that Dan Whiteley had been killed by the Chinese communists and had become a martyr, known to any student of the period?"

He waited for her to go on.

She said, still softly, "You are also so known. Tracy Cogswell, the dependable, the incorruptible, the organization man *plus ultra*, the indominable field man." She spoke as though reciting. "Fought in Spain in the International Brigades as a boy. Friend of George Orwell. Spent three years in Nazi concentration camps before escaping. Active in overthrowing Mussolini. Fought on the side of the Freedom Fighters in the Hungarian tragedy of 1956. Helped Djilas escape from Tito's dictatorship. Finally was given post of international secretary, coordinating activities from Tangier."

She took a deep breath before going on. "Captured by Franco's espionage-counterespionage agents and smuggled into Spain. Died under torture without betraying any members of the organization."

Tracy spilled his cup of coffee as he came to his feet. His voice was strained. "But . . . but Dan Whiteley was there, at the end. He knew that last wasn't true. I appropriated almost twenty thousand dollars of the movement's money. It must have been practically the whole international treasury, and that's why he had been sent to find out what in the hell was going on."

Jo Edmonds said with sour humor. "It would seem that your organization needed a martyr more than it needed a traitor or even the money. You've gone down in history as Tracy Cogswell, the incorruptible, the dependable, the perfect organization man."

Cogswell slumped back into his chair. At least in this fashion a hundred friends and comrades had never known his final act of betrayal. He hadn't been able to resist, but still it had been betrayal. Those friends and comrades he had fought shoulder to shoulder with to make a better world.

He said wearily, "All right. Now we come to the question that counts." He looked from one face to the other. They obviously knew what he was about to ask. He asked it: "Why?"

Jo Edmonds, for once, slipped his piece of jade back into a pocket. He opened his mouth to speak, but Academician Stein quieted him with a shake of his head.

He said, "Let me do this, Jo. We're at the crux of the matter. How we put this now means success or failure of the whole project."

Tracy Cogswell was beginning to come to a boil. "What project, damn it?" he snapped.

"Just a minute," Stein said, flustered a bit, obviously not used to dealing with persons in extreme anger. "Let me give you some background."

Tracy Cogswell snapped, "I've been getting background for days. Tell me why I'm here!"

The other was upset. "A moment please, Tracy . . . I'm going to call you Tracy . . . man was an aggressive, hard-fighting animal from the time he first emerged from the mists of antiquity. Physically weak, as predatory animals go, he depended on brains and cunning to subjugate his fellow beasts. Only those clever enough to outwit the sabertooth, the cave bear, the multitude of other beasts more dangerous physically than man, survived."

"Jesus Christ, I don't need this," Cogswell protested.

"A moment, please. You will see my reasons. Even when his fellow beasts were conquered, man still had nature to combat. He still had to feed, clothe, and shelter himself. He had to adjust to the seasons, protect himself during the cold and the night, floods and storms, of droughts and pestilences. And step by step he beat out his path of progress. It wasn't always easy, Tracy."

"It was never easy," Cogswell growled impatiently.

"All along the way," Stein continued, "man fought not only as a species but as an individual. Each man battled not only nature, but his fellow man as well, since there was seldom enough for all. Particularly when we get to the historic period and the emergence of the priest and the warrior and finally the noble: Man was pitted against his fellows for a place at the top. There was room there for only a small number."

The academician shook his head. "Survival of the fittest," he said. "Which often meant, under the circumstances, the most brutal, the most cunning, the conscienceless. But it also meant the strengthening of the race. When a ruling class was no longer the most aggressive and intelligent element of a people, it didn't long remain the ruling class."

Walter Stein hesitated for a long moment. "In short, Tracy, all through history man has had something to fight for . . . or against." He twisted his mouth in a grimace of attempted humor. "It's the nature of the beast."

"Isn't all this elementary?" Cogswell said. Some of the heat of his impatience was gone, but he still couldn't understand what the other was building up to.

The other said, uncertainly, "I suppose the first signs of it were evident even in your own period. I recall reading of educators and social scientists who began remarking on the trend before the twentieth century was halfway through. Remarking on it and bewailing it."

"What trend?" Cogswell scowled.

"In the more advanced countries of your period. The young people. They stopped taking the science and engineering courses in school; they considered them too difficult to bother with. A youngster didn't have to fight to make his way; the way was greased. The important thing was to have a good time. Find an angle so that you could obtain the material things everyone else had, without the expenditure of much effort. Don't

be an egghead. Don't stick your neck out. Conform.
You've got cradle to the grave security. Take it easy.
You've got it made.''

''Some went to the other extreme,'' Tracy said unhappily. ''They dropped out completely. Left school.
Didn't care about the material things. The boys grew
beards and long hair, the girls didn't give a damn what
they looked like. Most of them used marijuana or even
harder drugs. At first they were known as beats, or
beatniks. Later they started calling them hippies. What
was the term? . . . 'Rebels without a cause.' ''

Betty Stein, who had been silent for a long time, said
softly. ''And the most advanced countries . . . so far
as social progress was concerned, countries like Denmark and Sweden . . . had the highest suicide rates in
the world.''

''That's the point,'' Stein nodded. ''They had nothing to fight against and man is a fighting animal. Take
away something to work for, to fight for, and he's a
frustrated animal.''

A horrible understanding was growing within Tracy
Cogswell. He looked from one to the other of them,
almost desperately.

He said, ''What did you bring me here for?'' And his
voice was hoarse.

Academician Stein ignored him and pressed on.
''Since the success of your movement, Tracy Cogswell, there has been world government. Wars and ra-
cial tensions have disappeared. There is abundance for
all, crime is a thing of the past. Government, if you can
call it that, is so changed as hardly to be recognizable

from the viewpoint of your day. There are no politics, as you knew them.''

Jo Edmonds said bitterly, ''You asked about space flight yesterday. Sure, there are a couple of small bases on the moon, unmanned bases, automated bases, but nothing new has been done in the field for a generation. We have lots of dilettantes''—he flicked his beautifully carved bit of jade—''lots of connoisseurs, lots of gourmets . . . but few of us can bother to become scientists, builders, visionaries.''

''Why did you bring me here!'' Cogswell repeated.

''Because we need your know-how,'' Edmonds said flatly. He seemed a far cry from his usual easygoing self.

Cogswell's eyes became tired-looking. ''My know-how?''

Betty said gently, ''Tracy, when we sought back through history for someone to show us the way, we found Tracy Cogswell, the incorruptable, the dependable, the lifelong, devoted organization man.''

Tracy Cogswell was staring at her. ''Who are you people?'' he said. ''What's your angle?''

It was Academician Stein who answered, and he said what Cogswell now already knew. ''We're members of a new underground. The human race is turning to mush, Tracy. Something must be done. For more than half a century we've had what every Utopian through history has dreamed of. Democracy in its most ultimate form. Abundance for all. The end of strife between nations, races, and, for all practical purposes, between individuals. And, as a species, we're heading for dissolution. Tracy Cogswell, we need your experience to guide us. To overthrow the present socioeconomic system and form a new society.''

Edmonds leaned forward and put it in another way.

''You . . . and your movement . . . got us into this. Now get us out.''

Part Two

COUNTERREVOLUTION

Chapter One

Tracy Cogswell sent his disbelieving eyes from Academician Stein, to his daughter, to Jo Edmonds.

He said, "Are you all completely around the bend? You sit here and tell me you've pulled me through almost a century of time. You tell me that you suspended animation in me, or whatever you want to call it. That you, against my will, captured my brain, through some god-awful technique that you have developed, and made me steal some twenty thousand dollars, betray my friends, betray comrades who had many a time risked their lives for me. Betray everything I stood for. And now . . ."

Academician Stein was distressed. "Please Tracy. You are still much too weak. Don't strain yourself. We have been premature in allowing this to be brought up so soon."

"Strain myself!" Tracy glared at him. "Here you tell me that everything I've fought for all my life has been achieved. The human race, at long last, has abundance, no war; disease is practically wiped out. No crime. No race problems . . . Now you ask me to join your organization to overthrow all this. The things I've always dreamed of.'' His voice was so high it was all but shrill. ''My father before me was a revolutionist. After he died, in a vicious mining strike, my mother raised me in his tradition. Now you want me to help tear down everything he stood for. My great grandfather was an abolitionist. He died in the Civil War thinking he was helping to free the slaves.'' He laughed bitterly. ''A hell of a lot of slave freeing was done. The poor bastards just went from one type of slavery to another.''

''Please, Tracy,'' Betty said with anxiety in her voice. ''You're overwrought.''

He looked at her and there was a certain self-deprecation in his expression. He leveled his voice. ''I suppose that I'm not being very coherent.''

Edmonds had his jade piece out and was flipping it, over and over again. He said in his usual mild way, ''Hardly surprising under the circumstances, old chap.''

What was there about the guy that continually irritated Tracy? Well, it didn't make much difference. There was no particular reason for him to like him.

Cogswell looked at Academician Stein. ''I'm getting out of here. Because of you, I appropriated twenty thousand dollars which wasn't mine, though it was in my name. I want it back, Stein. I'll probably need it before I get organized in this new society of yours.''

Betty Stein said, ''Tracy, Tracy. I told you. We simply don't use money any more. If there was twenty thousand dollars, or twenty thousand of any other kind

60

of currency for that matter, it would probably be in some museum where people would stare at it in amazement that there could ever have been such things.''

He was impatient with her. ''Well, whatever the equivalent is. Credits, or whatever. You must have some sort of credit cards or whatever.''

Edmonds said, ''Why?''

Tracy glared at him. ''Suppose you want to go into a store and buy something.''

Edmonds flipped his piece of jade again and said mildly, ''It's fortunate that all three of us went to a lot of research on your period, I shouldn't wonder. Otherwise, half of the time we wouldn't know what you were talking about. You see, old chap, we don't have stores any more. Not in the sense you're talking about.''

Tracy closed his eyes momentarily. He opened them again and said. ''No stores, eh? All right. Suppose I wanted some clothes. Which is exactly one of the first things I'm going to want when I get out of here. How would I go about getting them?''

Walter Stein said, ''You would simply dial the distribution center in Tangier and order them. See here, Tracy, as your physician——''

''How would I pay for them?''

''You wouldn't,'' Edmonds said, as though reasonably. ''No need to, don't you know.''

Tracy glared at him again. ''Oh, I wouldn't, eh? They'd be for free, eh?''

''Yes.''

Tracy shook his head in despair. ''I don't seem to get

it. When I was working in the movement, we commonly believed that given a sane system of society we would be able to produce an abundance for all. But everything wasn't going to be *free*. Everybody was going to have to work. You'd do your share and you'd get your share. I think it was a guy named Herman Kahn, in a book about the year 2000, who predicted that by that time we'd have a per capita product worth something like $10,000 a year, and an average family income of $20,000."

"Failure of nerve and imagination," Edmonds murmured. "Most of those who tried to extrapolate at that time had similar trouble."

Academician Stein was making worried motions with his hands to quiet things down. He said, "Look here, Tracy Cogswell. I thought that we had made clear to you that the world today produces an absolute abundance for everyone."

"There's a limit to everything. Everything just can't be free."

"Tracy, Tracy," Betty said. "You can only eat three or four meals a day, even if you're a glutton. You can only wear one outfit of clothes at a time. You can only sleep in one bed. You can only ride in one vehicle at a time. You can only live in one house at a time. All of these things we have in abundance. Plenty of them for everybody."

"All right, all right," he said impatiently. "For that sort of thing, okay. But suppose I dialed this distribution center, or whatever you called it, and ordered all the diamonds they had in stock. Would they be free?"

"Diamonds?" Edmonds said blankly.

Betty said, "What in heavens would you want with diamonds?"

He looked at her in exasperation. "Diamonds, diamonds. Flawless blue diamonds. One of the most valuable things in the world."

"Oh," Edmonds said. "Of course. They used to be. Gems. Rubies, sapphires, uh, emeralds. That sort of thing, what? Jewelry." He looked over at Betty. "You know. Women used to wear it. Status symbols. That sort of thing." He turned his eyes back to the impatient Cogswell. "Women don't wear jewelry much any more. I doubt if there would be any diamonds at the local distribution center but if you wanted some they certainly wouldn't take more than twenty-four hours to manufacture you as many as you wanted."

"Manufacture?"

The other nodded. "Yes, certainly. If I remember correctly, a diamond is a pure or nearly pure form of carbon, crystalized in the isometric system. I believe that in the old days they were useful as points to tools due to their hardness. However, we now have artificial substances that are considerably harder, so diamonds are no longer utilized. Of course, another factor is that they were quite rare and difficult to locate and to mine." He frowned and added, "It seems to me that even in your day they were already beginning to manufacture diamonds, weren't they?"

Tracy gave up. He sighed and said, "Now that you mention it, I think they were able to produce small industrial diamonds. They had to subject carbon to extreme heat and pressure, or something. Damn it. They were beautiful! Precious! That's why people wanted them.''

"No they weren't,'' Betty said decisively. "I've seen some of the old jewelry in museums. The former British crown jewels, for instance. Gaudy, garish. And from twenty feet away you couldn't have told the difference between a diamond and a cleverly cut piece of glass or rhinestone. It would take an expert up close with his equipment to tell a flawed diamond from an unflawed one. Jo is right. They were status symbols, a symbol of wealth. Oh, some gems had a beauty of their own. Opals, star sapphires, jade, turquoise, but, as I recall, none of those were particularly precious. They were sort of semiprecious.''

Cogswell was frustrated. "All right. I shouldn't have picked jewelry for my example. But this matter of everything being free. Suppose I dialed this super-supermarket of yours and had them deliver a Rembrandt.''

Stein said, still soothingly, as though to calm his patient, "You mean the artist?''

"Yes, I mean the artist. Don't tell me you no longer look at paintings.''

The Academician said, "Oh, most certainly we do. We're very art conscious. Certainly you've noted the many we have in the house. Rembrandt is not a particular favorite of mine; however, if I wanted a reproduction of any of his . . .''

Cogswell had him now. "I wasn't talking about a reproduction,'' he said. "I was talking about an original Rembrandt. The real thing.''

The other shook his head in despair. He said, "You didn't have duplicators in your day, did you?"

"Duplicator?"

The Academician nodded. "Tracy Cogswell, today we have equipment that . . . well, we can take the Rembrandt painting you wish and so duplicate it that Rembrandt himself would not know the difference between the original and the copy. It would be *exactly* the same, down to practically the last molecule in the paint. And then you could make a copy of the copy and a copy of that and they would all be exactly alike . . . down to the last molecule."

"So why would you want the original?" Betty said in a reasonable tone." She thought about it. "Come to think, I doubt if anyone knows where any of the originals of a painter as famous as Rembrandt might be. Everything he ever did has been copied over and over again, probably thousands of times. How could you ever find the original?" Her expression indicated that the question had never crossed her mind before.

Tracy gave up. "The hell with it," he said. "At any rate, I'm getting out of here. All I want from you three is a little knowledge of the ropes. How I get a room in a hotel. How I get food in a restaurant. How I order from these distribution centers. I think that you owe me at least that much."

Jo Edmonds flipped his piece of jade and said softly, "Where would you go?"

"I don't know," Tracy said. "Somewhere to get orientated until I can get a job."

Walter Stein said, his voice still placating, "Tracy Cogswell, there are no jobs."

Tracy was scornful of that opinion. He said, "I'll find something. I'm no bum. You mean there's a lot of unemployment? I thought this was Utopia."

The academician sighed. He said, "Unemployment isn't quite the way to put it, Tracy Cogswell. Did you ever hear of a Dr. Richard Bellman of the Rand Corporation? Possibly he came after your time, I don't quite remember. At any rate, he predicted that by the end of the twentieth century two percent of the labor force would be able to produce all the products the United States could consume. Obviously, the rest of the developed nations were in much the same position."

"Once again, failure of nerve and imagination," Edmonds put in. "He failed to realize the extent to which automation and the computer, not to speak of nuclear fussion and other breakthroughs, would take over."

Tracy was staring again. He said, in utter disbelief, "You mean nobody works?"

Edmonds shrugged. "For all practical purposes, nobody has to work. Even those who do are usually employed at make-work projects. They wouldn't have to if they didn't want to."

Tracy *had* to reject that one. It was just out of the question. He said, "That's crazy! There'll always be *some* work that has to be done."

Stein nodded agreement to that and said, "Yes, and always some compulsive workers available to do it. But for all practical purposes labor has been eliminated. Machines do it so very much better."

Tracy Cogswell slumped back in his chair. So many

curves had been thrown at him in the past hour or so that he simply couldn't assimilate them.

The academician said, "Tracy Cogswell, it's what we told you. The human race is turning to mush. It no longer has purpose." He chuckled, but this time bitterly. "They used to think that the Romans went to pot because they gave their people free bread and circuses. Ha! Bread and circuses. In our age, we give our people everything free."

Tracy squared his shoulders and said, "All right, so be it, but I'm not your patsy. I'm clearing out of here just as soon as I can."

"Where would you go?" Edmonds repeated.

Tracy again glared at the younger man. He said, "What difference does it make to you?"

"You don't even speak the language," Jo said mildly. "And it makes a difference to me since I have been working with the academician on this project for several years now."

Cogswell laughed at him. "You haven't studied up on my background as much as you claim you have. I speak—besides my native English—French, Spanish, Italian, German and even have a smattering of Slavic. What language is current in these parts?"

Edmonds said smoothly, "Your languages are understood only by scholars, these days, Cogswell. How are you on Interlingua?"

Chapter Two

Tracy Cogswell looked from one of them to the other. Another curve had been thrown. "Interlingua?" he said.

"The international language," Betty explained. "Everybody speaks it now."

That floored him. He said, "You mean nobody speaks English, French, Spanish?"

She shook her head, as though sorry she had to tell him. "Only scholars of linguistics."

He said, "But . . . well, what was wrong with English? It was rapidly becoming more or less an international language. Practically all educated people spoke it everywhere. All the airlines . . . at least in the West . . . used it. And all ships used it in going through the red tape of leaving or entering a port. It . . ."

Betty took over the explaining. "English, like all the other languages before Interlingua, was a bastard tongue, Tracy. Consider its history, for a moment. When Caesar's Romans arrived, the language spoken in England was Celtic. The Romans, in their several centuries of occupation, grafted Latin on it. When they left, the waves of Saxons and Angelos occupied the country, followed by Danes and Norwegians, all with their own languages. Next came William the Conqueror an his Norman French. So you can see what I mean by a bastard language. Interlingua is a scientific language based on the earlier Esperanto and is more suited for a scientific society than yours was. To take just one or two examples, look at the way you form the plural in English.''

Tracy said, ''You simply add an 's.' ''

She shook her head, and said, ''Sometimes. Sometimes not. What is the plural of man? Mans? What is the plural of woman? Womans? And how do you form the feminine in English? By simply adding 'ess'? Sometimes, such as heir-heiress. But you can't say horse-horseess, or bull-bulless. You have to say mare and cow and you have to say boar-sow. There are no such exceptions in Interlingua. There are only a half-dozen grammatical rules, where in your day you had to study a whole book on grammar, and spelling is completely phonetic. It's easily learned, internationally understood. The most remote inhabitant of Mongolia speaks Interlingua.''

Cogswell thought about it after taking a deep breath.

Betty came to her feet and cleared up the breakfast things, put them on a tray and headed for the kitchen.

Apropos of nothing, Tracy muttered, ''So even in Utopia, a woman's work is never done.''

The academician frowned, not getting it at all. ''How do you mean?''

Tracy smiled at him. "Your daughter has gone to wash the dishes."

Edmonds laughed softly.

Tracy said to him, "What's so damn funny? In my time women were beginning to revolt against such things as kitchen drudgery."

Walter Stein said, "Tracy Cogswell, we don't wash dishes anymore."

Tracy scowled at him. "What do you do with them, just throw them away?"

"Yes. Or, at least, we throw them into the disposal unit. They are then recycled. The manner in which you utilized dishes and utensils, in your day, is now considered unsanitary. It was somewhat analogous to the way you washed and cleaned clothing."

"Oh, come on now, for Christ's sake. Are you suggesting that these days when a shirt or dress gets dirty you throw it away?" Tracy scoffed.

Stein nodded. "Yes, or any other article of clothing. In your day you washed it, ironed it, replaced any lost buttons, patched up any tears or holes, and stored it away for future use, taking up quite a bit of room in drawers or in a closet. We find that we save labor by throwing a garment away."

Tracy Cogswell was indignant. "That's one hell of a waste!"

The other shook his head before saying, "No, it isn't. The material is recycled and a brand new garment made available. Each morning we dial fresh clothing from the local distribution center."

Tracy gave it up. He said, "All right. The hell with

this. Tell me, how come you three people speak English if it's no longer in common use?"

"We studied it so that we could communicate with you, Tracy. We have been preparing for your coming for a long time."

"This story isn't holding up too well," Tracy said. "You say that you want my know-how to lead an underground revolt against the present socioeconomic system. How in the hell could I, if I don't even speak the language?"

Betty had returned and now resumed her chair, smiling at Tracy in what he assumed to be reassurance.

Jo Edmonds said, in his usual lazy tone, "We planned on teaching you Interlingua."

Tracy grunted before saying, "It'd take a coon's age for me to pick up a new language to the point I could communicate in such a field as socioeconomics, be able to give speeches, write pamphlets and so forth. I'm not a kid any longer. Fifteen or twenty years ago, I used to be a whiz at it. I could pick up a smattering of a language in a month, and be really fluent in a year."

"Less than a week," Edmonds said mildly.

"A week? You mean you figure on teaching me a language that I've never even heard of before in a week's time? Don't be ridiculous."

The academician cleared his throat and said, "Tracy, there have been changes in education since you went into, ah, hibernation."

Tracy snorted at that. He said, "There sure as hell would have to be."

The other sighed and said, "Let me give you a bit of

71

background. Do you remember a certain Dr. Robert Oppenheimer in your times?''

''Sure,'' Tracy said. ''He was the one who headed the nuclear fission team that produced the A-bomb.''

''Yes. He was a very competent physicist.''

Tracy accepted that but said, ''And a damn fool when it came to political economy.''

''Perhaps,'' the other agreed. ''However, what I was getting at was that in 1955, not long before we took over your body, he made the statement that human knowledge was doubling every eight years. Let us suppose that he made his calculation beginning the year 1945 using the old calendar.''

Tracy scowled. ''What do you mean, the old calendar? I think you mentioned that before. What kind of calendar do you use now?''

Betty took up the ball. She said, ''We changed at the beginning of the year 2000. You see, the old calendar was inaccurate. Even the Mayans had devised one more accurate than the one Europeans had utilized since the Middle Ages. Besides, a dozen or more different calendars were being used. The Moslems, for instance, based theirs on the moon, rather than the sun. Every year they lost a day or two. The Chinese utilized still a different system. Obviously, all this was pure nonsense when a world government took over. I'll explain it all to you some other time. It is now the year 45 New Calendar.''

The academician took over again, saying, ''At any rate, a century has passed since 1945. A century which started off with human knowledge doubling every eight years.''

"Jesus Christ," Tracy said, as some of the ramifications came through.

The other nodded. "Yes, had the pace continued, we would now have approximately eight thousand times as much knowledge as the race possessed a century ago."

"But it hasn't continued?" Tracy's voice was puzzled.

Edmonds dropped his jade piece into a pocket and said, "That's what we've been telling you, Cogswell. The race has turned to mush. Practically nobody gives a shit any more, to use the picturesque old-time idiom."

Tracy turned back to the older man. He scowled and said, "Well . . . what's all this got to do with my learning Interlingua in less than a week. Hell, I haven't been in a school for twenty years." He snorted in sour amusement when he realized all over again where and when he was. "I take that back. A hundred and twenty years."

Betty said softly, "Uh, Tracy, you see we don't have schools any more."

He couldn't think of anything to say to that. He simply stared at her in disbelief.

Her father said hurriedly, "Not in the old sense of the word, Tracy. That is, school rooms and all. You see, we've gone beyond them."

Tracy was flabbergasted. He said, "How in the hell can you go beyond schools? How do the kids learn to read and write? We've had schools since way back in Egyptian times."

The old man twisted his face as though trying to put words together that would give clarity. He said, "I think the first person to state the problem was a writer of your period named Arthur C. Clarke. He, himself, had possibly one of the most universal brains of the time, but he saw the coming problem. He pointed out that already twenty years of school were insufficient and that civilization would not be able to continue without some form of what he called a 'mechanical educator' which would be able to impress on the brain in a matter of a few minutes knowledge and skills which might ordinarily take a lifetime to acquire. Otherwise, he said, we could get to the point where we would die of old age before having learned to live, and the entire culture would collapse owing to its incomprehensive complexity.''

"Holy smokes," Tracy blurted. "You mean that you've got such a machine?"

The academician shook his head. He said, "Not exactly. We can't do it in a matter of minutes, but utilizing our autoteachers and certain chemical stimulants, we can most certainly teach you Interligua in less than a week."

Tracy was amazed. "But, good God, with a thing like . . . why, you mean that I could study some subject like, say, physics and in a few weeks know everything there was to know about it?"

Jo Edmonds said in the mild voice that was his wont, "Are you particularly interested in physics, old chap?"

Tracy looked at him. The other had his piece of jade out again. "Well, no," he said.

"Neither am I. Why clutter your head up with it? I'm not interested in cooking, either, beyond the eating of it. Why in the world should I cram a Cordon Bleu chef's know-how into my poor skull?"

74

"Jesus Christ," Tracy said meaninglessly.

Betty came to her feet decisively. "All well and good, but we could sit here for the rest of the week and never answer all the questions Tracy could ask. I suggest that he and I go into the study, and he can get at his Interlingua. No matter what he finally decides about helping our group, he's going to have to learn the language even to cope with everyday problems."

Tracy said, "But there are a lot of things——"

"They can wait," Betty said. "Even if you are anxious to get off and away, away from us, it's going to take you a week of study . . . and probably that much to completely regain your strength."

"Yes," her father said. "You are in no condition to leave my supervision, Tracy Cogswell. I am surprised that you have been able to go through the emotional strain you have been under this morning."

"I've been through emotional strain before," Tracy growled, but he came to his feet and looked at the girl to lead the way.

They left the breakfast nook, and Tracy followed her to his room and beyond it to another chamber which he hadn't been in before. It was well supplied with windows that looked out over the straits so that it was well lit. It had a double shelf of books along one wall and was furnished with a large desk and two chairs, one a swivel chair behind the desk, the other a comfortable looking overstuffed affair.

"This will be your study," Betty said. "We readied it for you long before father ever brought you out of hibernation."

He wanted to say something to the effect that they'd

been awfully sure of themselves, but he realized that what she had said earlier was quite valid. Until he at least got to know the language, there was no place for him to go to that would make sense.

She went over to the desk and pointed out two screens which to him looked like nothing so much as ordinary medium-sized television screens.

Betty Stein began giving him directions about the equipment. "This is your autoteacher," she told him. "This is how you activate it, with this switch. It's connected to the Universal Data Banks and——"

"What are the Universal Data Banks?"

She said, "The world library, the world archives, world statistics. All the knowledge that the world has accumulated down through the centuries."

He looked at her as though she was putting him on.

But she shook her head and said patiently, "Tracy you were already in hibernation when Watershed Week came along. It happened in a week of July 1969. All the computer people in the world knew it was coming and were waiting for it. Some of them held sort of reverse celebrations, since the implications were somewhat frightening."

"What in the devil was Watershed Week?"

She said, "That was the week in which for the first time the information-handling capacity of all the computers in the world exceeded the information-handling capacity of all the human brains in the world. In short, the computers were able to receive and store more information than the three and a half billion human brains that there were on Earth at that time. By 1975

Old Calendar the computers had more than fifty times the capacity of humanity."

Tracy Cogswell couldn't quite comprehend. He said, "What does that have to do with having all the information in the world in this one big overgrown library?"

She said patiently, "I suppose it must have started as far back as your time . . . possibly a little later. They began by putting statistics into the computer data banks, at first dealing with income tax and such things. It quickly became so practical that other information was filed away. I believe it was some town in California which first hit upon the idea of so recording all pertinent information on all of its citizens. Not long after, the FBI put all its criminal records into its data banks. This was so practical that local and state police cooperated and submitted their files on criminals."

"Talk about Big Brother," Tracy muttered.

She went on, saying, "A more popular step was when all medical records went into what were now the National Data Banks of the United States, which was far in advance of all other countries in the booming computer revolution. About this time, some genius of forethought came up with the idea of storing in the data banks all of the books in the Library of Congress. And shortly afterwards all the books in all of the libraries, including those of the universities. When practical computer translators were finally developed, this was extended first to the British Museum library, then that of the Sorbonne in Paris, and to the Vatican Library in Rome. By the time world government came along, the now International Data Banks were thrown open to all libraries in all languages. Filed away in the banks were every book ever written, every newspaper published . . . for that matter, every bit of music, every painting.''

"For Christ's sake," Tracy protested. "How could you ever find anything?"

"It's all cross-indexed a score of ways," she smiled wryly. "It's pretty well worked out by now. I'll tell you more about it some other time, but for now shall we get about our business?"

She sat down at the desk behind the screens, opened a desk drawer, and brought forth a book that reminded Tracy of a telephone book of a large city of his own time.

She said, "Now here are our categories. First we dial for Education. Under that we dial Language. And, under that, Interlingua. Under that we dial Elementary Interlingua. And under that, Volume One, Chapter One. Here. You sit here behind the screen.

She came to her feet to make room for him and moved to one side and reached down into the desk drawer again, as he seated himself unhappily.

"What happens now?" he said. A book had manifested itself on the screen before him: Elementary Interlingua, Volume I.

She came up with a small bottle, unscrewed the top and shook a pill into her hand. "Now you take your stimmy," she told him.

"What's a stimmy?"

"A mental stimulant. It effects both your IQ and your retentive abilities."

There was a carafe of water and a glass on the desk. She poured him a drink and handed over glass and pill.

He shrugged and took it and washed it down. "How long does it take to work?" he said. "And how long will it continue to be effective?"

"A few minutes to work and it will last about an hour," she told him. "If you want to continue to study after that time, you simply take another one."

"Why doesn't everybody take them all of the time?"

"You'll see," she said wryly. "Now this button here flips the pages for you. This one here will reverse pages if there is any reason for you to go back and check something. See how I press this to bring you to Page One, Chapter One?"

Tracy said grudgingly, "With gismos like this, I can see why you no longer have schools. I'd think that just about everybody would be cramming themselves with scores of subjects."

She said lowly, "It's as Jo said. Most people don't give a damn. All they're interested in is hedonism . . . having a good time."

Something suddenly happened. He speed-read the first page and realized that he understood it completely. Then, for a moment he gaped. He darted a look at Betty Stein. Very very slowly, as though in a movie slow motion, she was walking toward the armchair. She slowly, slowly turned and seemingly took a full minute to seat herself.

She smiled and said, very very slowly, "If . . . you . . . have . . . finished . . . that . . . first . . . page . . . press . . . the . . . button."

Now he could see why everybody didn't take stim-mies all of the time. The world, save for him, had slowed down, or he had sped up . . . or both. It would be no way to go through life. He pressed the page-flipping button and went back to work.

Chapter Three

About two hours later and when the effects of Tracy's second stimmy were about worn off, Academician Stein came in. As usual, his expression was of worry, undoubtedly about his patient. Betty was still seated in her chair. The second time she had taken a stimmy herself, the better to answer questions of the new student in regard to such matters as pronunciation, although theoretically the autoteacher was giving him that.

The academician looked at Tracy and said, *"Kiel vi fartas?"*

Tracy was already up to that one but not happy about his accent enough to answer in Interlingua. He said, "I suppose that I'm doing okay. This machine is the damnedest thing I've ever run into."

Stein turned to his daughter. *"Kiun libron li legas,"* he said to her in Interlingua.

Tracy said, "Damn it. Let's stick to English until I get a little further along."

Betty said to her father, "He's still on the first

volume of Elementary Interlingua but he's about half through.''

"In two hours? Excellent. Jo Edmonds was wrong. It will take quite a bit less than a week for him to learn adequate Interlingua.''

Betty raised and lowered one shapely shoulder. "Adequate for everyday usage, yes. But, as Tracy pointed out, he's got to be able to communicate intelligently in socioeconomics and related subjects. He has to be able to assimilate the history that has transpired since his day.''

"Like hell I do," Tracy said. "As soon as I can get along well enough for everyday living, I'm getting out of here. I don't buy your scheme to overthrow Utopia.''

"There is no such thing as Utopia," Stein said definitely. "It's something man strives for, runs after, but he never gets it in his grasp. As soon as he reaches one milepost, there's another. Right now, we're bogged down. We're not even trying to get to the next milepost.''

"It's your problem, not mine," Tracy told him stubbornly. "My age had another milepost to reach. You've now reached it. Where you go from here on in is your business. My business is through.''

The other said worriedly, "Tracy, I am afraid that you have overdone it. I suggest that you return to your room and stretch out for a time. I'll give you a sedative, if you wish. Rest a couple of hours until lunch.''

"I'm not tired. I'd like to get on with this. The sooner I learn it, the better.''

Stein shook his head. "I'm your physician. Your

strength will pick up quite rapidly from now on. But today, in particular, you've been under quite a bit of strain.''

"Okay." Tracy leaned back in his chair. "In just a minute." He looked at Betty and indicated the second screen on the desk. "You didn't explain this."

She said, "It's a second screen, also connected to the Universal Data Banks. Sometimes when you're studying you wish to consult another work at the same time. A reference book or something."

He said, "Suppose I want to consult three or four books, at the same time? In my day, sometimes a student would litter his whole desk with a half dozen books, open to this page or that, and check and recheck this passage or that."

Betty laughed. "Either of those screens will take four books at a time. "I'll show you how, on your next session."

He indicated the books in the two bookshelves. "How about those? If you've got everything in the data banks, why should you need any books at all?"

Walter Stein chuckled ruefully. "I'm afraid that I'm a compulsive underliner and marginal marker and commentator on books. Those are some of my favorites, so I've had them printed up and have filled them with my notations. I have others scattered about the house.''

"So you can get books if you want them, eh?"

"Certainly," the older man told him. "It's no problem at all. Just dial the distribution center and they'll have it done up for you."

Tracy was surprised. "You mean they'd just print up one book? Just for you?"

"Why yes. It's all automated, you know. It wouldn't take more than half an hour for you to have it in your hands. But now, off with you. Into bed!"

Tracy came to his feet, realizing suddenly that the other was right. He was tired. He didn't think he had ever gone through a period of his life in which he had assimilated so much that was new and strange to him as he had this morning.

He followed his host . . . if that was the term . . . and Betty into his bedroom-cum-hospital-room and kicked off his slippers and stretched out on the bed. Betty winked at him, and she and her father left. He still thought she looked like Paulette Goddard, though her hair was cut as short as Ingrid Bergman's when she had the part of Maria in *For Whom the Bell Tolls*.

But there was no nap. There had been too much thrown at him. He was too stirred up to even recapitulate it all. He fell into a semidoze of weariness, and some of it came back to him.

Dan Whiteley. Dan had been, Tracy supposed, his best friend, in a world in which Tracy Cogswell had not had a good many friends. He had never had the time to accumulate friends. Close comrades, yes, or rather close companions, members of the organization who would have died for him in the clutch, or he for them. He didn't like the word *comrade*. Too many people identified it with the Commies, and if people connected you with the Commies, that was the kiss of death, so far as recruiting them to your cause was concerned. The

Commies had alienated just about every thinking person in the world by the time Stein had taken over his mind and body.

But Dan Whiteley, yes, and Bud Whiteley, his brother. He had met the two of them in the Abraham Lincoln Battalion. They were actually Canadians, not Americans; there had been quite a few Canadians in the outfit. It and the George Washington Battalion had been formed slightly before the Canadian Mackenzie-Papineau Battalion. All of them and the Dimitrov, which was Yugoslavian, and the British Battalion, and the French Sixth of February Battalion, went up to make the Fifteenth Brigade. There had been seven of the International Brigades in all; battalions composed of Germans, Belgians, Poles, Hungarians, other Balkans, Czechs, Bulgarians, and even Albanians. In all, twenty-nine nations had been represented. Tracy had even met an Abyssinian and a Jamaican. And practically all had been wiped out. The Stalinists, once they were in power in Spain, had used them for shock troops, had thrown them in whenever things were going badly. The brigades had too many independent thinking members for the Commies to like them around. They might throw a monkey wrench in some of Uncle Joe Stalin's double-dealings.

Yes, the Spanish Civil War—testing ground for Germany and Italy on one side, and for the Soviets on the other. Poor Spain had been in between. Poor Spain and the thousands of young men who had come from all over the world to fight for what they thought was democracy.

"Democracy, ha!" Tracy snorted. There had been about as much democracy on one side as the other.

Tracy had still been in high school in Cincinnati when Franco's Spanish Foreign Legion and Moroccan troops had been airlifted across from Spanish Morocco by German Junkers, some twenty thousand of them in all. It was the first airlift in history, and Hitler was probably right when he said later that "Franco ought to erect a monument to the glory of the Junkers fifty-two. It is this aircraft that the Spanish Revolution has to thank for its victory."

At any rate, the Spanish Civil War was on and from the first Tracy, though only seventeen at the time, was fascinated. It was in the middle of the depression in the States and a good many of his fellow students belonged to one liberal or radical group or the other; Socialists, Communists, technocrats, there was even a branch of the Trotskyites. Tracy didn't belong to any of them but he preferred even the Soviets to Hitler and Mussolini, and it soon became obvious that Germany and Italy were backing Franco against the Spanish Republic.

When the International Brigades began to form, he left a note for his aging parents and hitchhiked to New York and located the recruiting office of the American Abraham Lincoln Battalion. It had some high-flown title such as the American Committee For the Aid of the Spanish Republic, but later on he was told by Dan Whiteley that it was a Commie front organization. At any rate, they saw to his getting a passport and a third-class passage to France. He travelled with nine others, one of whom was from Montreal and spoke

French and was theoretically in charge for the time. They disembarked in Le Havre and took the train to Paris where they were met by a representative of the Spanish government and shipped, after two nights on the town, along with twenty or so others, to Ceret in the foothills of the Pyrenees.

At this time, the French were already taking a dim view of the international volunteers who were crossing their borders into Spain. Consequently, that night the whole group took off, by foot, led by a Spaniard who had been sent over for them. They crossed the border over mountain passes as though they had been smugglers. They walked all the way to the town of Figueras, on the rail line running from Port-Vendres, France, to Barcelona, and took the first train into the Catalonian capital.

In Barcelona the authorities thoughtfully relieved the new recruits of their passports. Cogswell was to learn later that these were turned over to the Russian KGB, who utilized them in international espionage-counterespionage. Not having a passport made things difficult when he was working his way back home, two years later.

They trained at the village of Villanueva de la Jara, near Albacete, and it was here the Americans realized their disadvantage. The draft was a thing of the future in the States. Few of them had even been in the American National Guard. The European volunteers had almost all served in the armies of their native lands and some were combat veterans. Six of the Italians had been in the invasion of Ethiopia, and others, mostly Germans, had served a hitch in the French Foreign Legion. Some of the older men had participated in World War I. Most of the veterans were immediately made noncoms.

The Americans were largely students and largely city bred. Their average age was considerably younger than that of the Europeans; Tracy was youngest of all. He had lied when he told them he was twenty in New York. His 'military experience' consisted of having belonged to the Boy Scouts for two years. His experience with firearms consisted of hunting rabbits and squirrels in southern Indiana and northern Kentucky with a twenty-two.

At Villanueva de la Jara, Tracy was issued the standard Spanish uniform, which consisted of a cap rather than a helmet, a heavy shirt, and pants. Evidently, Spanish soldiers were not so effete as to wear underwear. He kept his own shoes, which luckily were heavy; they were his hiking footwear. The Republic was short of boots in those days.

He was also issued a SMLE, which meant a short magazine Lee Enfield, probably left over from World War I; it fired the outdated .303 caliber cartridge and had a ten-round detachable box magazine. Where it had come from he hadn't the vaguest idea. He found later that the Republic was armed from a dozen different countries, including Germany and Italy, through Portugal, and the story was that a great deal of graft went into the securing of munitions. There was some American equipment, usually filtered in through Mexico, which, practically alone among the western nations, was in support of the Republic.

The training was minimal. There was a crisis in the vicinity of Madrid, which was already partially surrounded by the Fascist armies. They were rammed on through and sent off to join the International Brigades for which they had signed up.

They were in Madrid for only a single day and were then trucked that night to an unknown destination. The rumor was that the Republicans were about to embark on a major offensive. But there have been rumors in the army since long before the days of Alexander the Macedonian. Are we going to India, or are we going to reverse our engines—or rather chariots, in those days—and take on that newly erupting, brash town, Rome?

He had hardly more than met Robert Merriman, the bespectacled twenty-eight-year-old commander of the Abraham Lincoln Battalion. Merriman was the son of a lumberjack who had worked his way through the University of Nevada and had become a lecturer at the University of California. The story was that he had come to Europe on a travelling scholarship to investigate agricultural problems, when the civil war broke out. He had immediately made his way to Spain. Later on he was to be made chief of staff of the 15th Brigade and was to die on the Ebro River where the International Brigades suffered heavy losses in the final days of the conflict.

Yes, the Ebro. Tracy Cogswell remembered the Ebro. They had fought their last action there on 22 September. Not only had Bob Merriman fallen there, after getting through the whole war, but also a kid not much older than Tracy himself, Jim Lardner, son of the American writer Ring Lardner and one of the last Americans to have enlisted. He had broken his glasses on the final day, and couldn't even see well enough to use his rifle.

But Tracy Cogswell shifted his bulk in the bed and brought his mind back to his first meeting with Dan and Bud Whiteley.

They had left in Madrid and headed north. There were trucks, armored cars, tanks, motorcycles, and occasional staff cars, strung out before and after, as far as he could see from the truck in which he and some twenty-five others sat or squatted. It was jammed to the gunnels. He was lucky to have gotten a bench seat up against the side.

It was night but they drove without lights. The faces of the men were expressionless, save for a certain sadness. There was no banter and, at first, very little talk at all. All they knew was that they were due for an attack and what the next few days held was in the lap of the gods.

The large trucks, all painted gray and with more than ordinary clearance, had high, square cabs and square, ugly radiators. Most of them had French 8mm M 1914 Hotchkiss machine guns mounted above the cab as antiaircraft defense.

The man next to Tracy looked at him and said, "You're one of the new replacements, aren't you? I don't believe I've seen you before."

"Yeah," Tracy said, hoping his voice didn't indicate his nervousness, his fear of what the following hours were to hold.

The other was a tall man, on the gangling side and possibly a few years older than Tracy. His mouth was too wide and he seemed to hold it in a perpetual half-grin. Light was insufficient for Tracy to make him out too well. He carried on his lap a submachine gun, with a heavy drum rather than a clip. Tracy didn't know it then but it was a Russian PPD 34 and fired the standard Soviet pistol round, the 7.62 rimless.

"Name's Whiteley," the other said. "Dan Whiteley."

"Cogswell. Tracy Cogswell." He couldn't think of anything else to say, so he said the usual. "Where you from, Dan?"

"Winnipeg."

"Where's Winnipeg?"

"Manitoba. It's the capital of Manitoba."

Tracy said, "I'm sorry. Where's Manitoba?"

The other laughed. "You Yanks," he said derisively. "I'll bet you don't even know what the capital of Canada is. The closest country to you and you know practically nothing about it."

Tracy was glad to have the opportunity to talk, to put his thoughts on something other than impending death. He said, defensively, "It's, uh, Toronto."

Whiteley laughed again. "It's Ottawa. The capital of the United States is Washington. Your president's name is Franklin Roosevelt. I'll bet you don't know our premier's name. Where do you come from?"

Tracy had him now, to his satisfaction. "Cross Plains," he said.

"Indiana?"

"I'll be damned. How did you know? The population can't be more than two or three hundred, counting cows.''

The other laughed again, pleased with himself. ''Pure chance. I drove through there a year or so ago, heading east to New York, and stopped off to see an old character named Wooley who had raised the biggest steer in North America. It was big as a barn.''

''I'll be damned,'' Tracy said. ''I knew Lon Wooley. But my family moved to Cincinnati when I was a kid.''

Dan Whiteley indicated the man at his right with a thumb. ''This is my brother, Bud. Hey, Buddy, meet Tracy Cogswell.''

Bud had been dozing, swaying gently to the monotonous movement of the troop carrier. If he hadn't he been packed in so tight between his brother and the man to his right, he undoubtedly would have fallen to the truck floor, or, at least, onto the men seated there.

He said, sleepily, ''Hi.''

Dan said, ''Bud's a bit hung over. It got a little drunk out yesterday, when we found out about this push.''

Tracy looked over. Bud Whiteley was possibly nineteen or twenty, considerably shorter than his brother, and heftier. His face was just now slack but Tracy suspected that even under the best of conditions it wasn't exactly intellectual. Easygoing would have been the better term. His ears stuck out like those of Bing Crosby. Tracy had read somewhere that they had to tape Crosby's ears down when he was in a movie, especially in a romantic scene. Dan Whiteley, on the other hand, looked more like Gary Cooper, back in the

92

days when Cooper was still a kid. What was that old movie he'd played in with Wallace Beery?

Tracy said, "Glad to meet you."

But Bud Whiteley had dozed off again.

Dan said, "This your first action?"

"Yeah."

"Whose squad are you in?"

Tracy said, "Damned if I know. I hardly more than got to Madrid than they put me in this truck."

"Then you're probably in mine," the other said. "If not, we'll make arrangements. Things are pretty informal in the brigades." Whiteley chuckled again. "Informal, shit. They're chaotic. At any rate, stick with Buddy and me. The first time you're under fire is bitchy. It scares the holy blue jazus out of you. Hell, any time you're under fire is bitchy. I still get scared."

A staff car came up from behind them, blasting with its Klaxon and flicking its lights off and on to clear the way. For the first time, Tracy could see Whiteley clearly. He was reassured by his appearance and came to the conclusion that he would be a good man to be with when the going scoured.

He said, "You're a sergeant?"

"That's right," Whiteley grinned. "And if the war lasts another year, knock on wood, I hope it doesn't, I'll be a damned colonel."

"How do you mean?"

"I mean that at the rate the brigades take casualties, promotion is fast. Anybody who can execute an about-face, and knows what end of the gun a slug issues from, is made a lieutenant."

"Oh," Tracy said unhappily. "You've already seen quite a bit of combat, eh?"

"Yeah," Whiteley answered. "But and I have been in it from the first. The first action this battalion saw. It was in the Jarama valley. The fascists wanted to cut the Madrid-to-Valencia road and caught us by surprise. For once, thank God, we had control of the air. The Russkies had brought in a whole slew of Moscas, kind of a Russian version of the American Boeing P32. Our battalion was stationed between Pingarron and San Martin, under that stupid son of a bitch Gal. Man, did we take a beating. We started out with four hundred fifty men and a hundred twenty were killed and a hundred seventy-five wounded. Even at that, we didn't do as bad as the British Battalion. They started out with six hundred and before the day was through only two hundred twenty-five were left." He paused a moment before adding, "But the fuckin' fascists didn't cut the road."

Tracy Cogswell hissed between his teeth. With casualty rates like that you had less than a fifty-fifty chance of getting through even a single engagement.

The other grinned again. "I told you promotion was quick in this war. Why? Because we lost practically every officer in the battalion. I went in as a private and came out a corporal."

He began singing, to the tune of "Red River Valley," and several of the others joined in.

"There's a valley in Spain called Jarama
It's a place that we all know too well,
For 'tis there that we wasted our manhood,
And most of our old age as well."

It was beginning to get light, and Tracy could see his companions better now. Bud Whiteley was shaking himself awake and running a coated tongue over coated lips distastefully.

Tracy looked at Dan Whiteley, taking in the insignia on his sleeve. "Corporal?" he said. "But you're a sergeant aren't you?"

Whiteley chuckled again; he was evidently a great one for grins and laughter. "Yeah. I told you I'd wind up a colonel if the war lasted another year. Jarama was in February. In March the Italians decided they'd capture Guadalajara and started out gung-ho with all their speedy Fiat tanks and their Fiat CR thirty-two pursuit planes for air cover. I wish the hell all armies were like the wops. There wouldn't be any more wars. Their battle cry is, 'I surrender,' and as soon as they spot an enemy they give the double fascist salute. Both hands high in the air."

Tracy had to laugh.

Whiteley continued, "At any rate, we killed off about two thousand of them and wounded something like four thousand and captured quite a few hundred. Then we chased them back a few miles and since we'd taken some casualties ourselves, especially among the noncoms, I wound up a sergeant."

Bud said sourly, "Now all we have to do is lose a couple of lieutenants."

Three aircraft, in tight formation, streaked over them, heading up the road.

Tracy's instinct was to hunch down, expecting bombs or machine gun fire.

But the others looked up without alarm and one of

them said, "Russian I-sixteens. The Spanish call them *chatos*, flat-nosed ones. At least we're having some air cover."

"We'll need it," one of those seated on the floor muttered glumly. "Do you know where we're going?"

Somebody else snorted and said, "Do you? This is supposed to be some big surprise."

"Surprise my ass," the other said. "For the last week they've been discussing the big government offensive in every sidewalk cafe in Madrid. Every goddamned fascist in Spain probably knows all about it."

One of those seated up front near the cab, a big Negro, said, "I heard we were going to take Brunete and roll up the fascists from the rear, all the way to Madrid."

"So did I," someone else growled. "And if we heard about it, you sure as hell know Franco's boys have."

Empty trucks, coming from the opposite direction, were becoming increasingly more numerous. And they passed a half dozen mud-colored tanks in a grove of trees. The tanks were covered with branches, in way of camouflage. Their 45-mm guns jutted out horizontally beyond them. The tank crews, gunners and drivers, wore ridged helmets and leather coats and were sitting around smoking, leaning up against tree trunks or sleeping on the ground.

"We're getting near the front," Dan Whiteley said. "Those tanks are probably in reserve. French Renaults. The wop Fiats are faster but not as heavily armed or armored. It's the goddamned German tanks that are the

AFTER UTOPIA

best. Even most of our antitank guns hardly dent them." He added grudgingly, "The Russians aren't bad either, but there's not enough of them. That son of a bitch Stalin sends us just enough to keep us going."

One of the men on the floor said, "You oughtn't to talk about Comrade Stalin like that."

"Fuck off, you stupid Commie."

They were beginning to hear the rumble of guns up ahead, a rumble that increased geometrically as they progressed. Then heavier explosions. Aircraft bombs?

Half a dozen large four-engined monoplanes flew over them at a considerably greater altitude than the fighters that had zipped over earlier.

Whiteley said, "Topolev TB-three bombers. Ours, again. They're better than the German three-motor Ju-fifty-two. Are you taking all this in?"

"What?" Tracy said.

"For Christ's sakes, you think I'm talking to hear myself talk? When I told you those were Renault tanks back there it was so you'd know one when you saw one. You have to know your own equipment as well as the enemy's. You have to know when to hit the dirt and when you don't have to."

The trucks ground to a halt and a shout came from up forward which Tracy didn't make out.

Dan Whiteley said, "Okay, men, this is it. Everybody pile out."

Throwing their packs before them, the men vaulted out over the tailboard and grouped to one side of the road, looking apprehensively in the direction of the explosions.

Dan Whiteley said, "Are any of the rest of you greenies?" He looked at one in particular. "I don't believe I've ever seen you before."

The soldier, who was gray of face and couldn't have been more than twenty, said, "Yeah, Sergeant, I came in just yesterday along with Tracy. Sidney Simon."

Whiteley said to the big Negro, "Jim, you and Harry take him under your wing."

"Sure thing," Jim said, and then to Simon, "You stick near to me, white boy."

It was becoming increasingly lighter. A small group of officers and noncoms were forming up ahead about a hundred yards and to one side of the road. Dan Whiteley trotted up to join them.

Jim said gloomily, staring off in the direction of the artillery fire, "I shoulda stood in Harlem."

The one Whiteley had called Harry said, "Why didn't you?"

Jim pretended to be indignant. "What'd'ya mean? I'm here fighting for mother-fucking democracy."

Dan Whiteley came back in about fifteen minutes, his face drawn. The group of officers had broken up and returned to their units.

Whiteley said, "All right. We're moving in. Crowd around and I'll tell you what little I know."

They gathered around him.

He said, "The rumors we heard in Madrid are right, damn it. We've got two army corps here under supreme command of Miaja. We're with the Fifth Corps under Modesto. The first objective is Brunete, which is about ten kilometers to the south. We've got to take it before

98

AFTER UTOPIA

the damned German Condor Legion can get down here
from the north with its heavy artillery. In front of us
we've got the Falangist Seventy-first Division and
about a thousand Moroccans.''

He looked in particular at Tracy and the other new
replacement named Simon and said, ''If it looks as
though you're going to be captured by Italians, okay.
By Spanish, okay. Even by Germans. But if it's
Moroccans, don't be.''

Tracy Cogswell said, confused, ''Well, what can
you do?''

Dan Whiteley looked at him. ''About fifty percent of
them are queer as chicken shit. For a nice boy like you,
who looks like he doesn't have to shave more than
about once a week, the message is, don't be captured by
the Moroccans.''

He looked around at the others. ''Any questions?''

Jim said, ''Yeah. Which way is Madrid? I'm going
over the hill.''

Some of the others laughed sourly, even as they took
up their packs, shrugged into them, and under
Whiteley's orders formed a ragged double rank. Bud
Whiteley and Tracy were side by side, immediately
behind Bud's brother. They began to trudge forward.
Behind them, the empty trucks were turning to head to
the rear.

Tracy was wounded in combat in the next three days.

As an infantryman, he had only a vague idea of what
was going on. It seemed mostly marching, counter-
marching, digging, hiding. He fired at the enemy and
was fired on, usually at quite a distance. He saw Jim

and Sidney go down in a burst of machine gun fire. Bud Whiteley lobbed a grenade into the machine gun nest, taking a hit in his own stomach as a result, since he had to expose himself. Two medics hauled him off in a stretcher. Dan Whiteley looked after him anxiously, but Bud only grinned.

It was a mess-up, Dan Whiteley told Cogswell. The battle, fought on the parched Castilian plain during the height of the summer, assumed a chaotic, bloody character. They took Brunete on schedule but then were thrown back when the Falangists brought in fresh elements, tanks and what seemed to be flocks of Heinkel He-51s of the Condor Legion. They didn't seem to have the speed and maneuverability of the Russian Chatos and Moscas, but they were all over the sky.

When the front finally stabilized with both sides dug in, the Republicans had gained an area five kilometers deep along a fifteen-mile front. They paid for it. The Abraham Lincoln Battalion and the George Washington Battalion took so many casualties that they had to be merged into one. The George Washington Battalion even lost their commander, Olive Law, a Negro excorporal of the U.S. Army. The British fared worse, and their battalion was reduced to eighty men.

Looking back at it from his present situation, Tracy wondered that he had ever survived the war. There had been some twenty-eight hundred Americans in all in the brigades and about nine-hundred of these were killed and at least an equal number were badly wounded. Bud Whiteley, who had recovered from his belly wound, had fallen on the Ebro only three days before the International Brigades had been pulled out and sent over the border into France. There were only fifty-four on hand to leave. Some of the others had refused to go and remained to fight in Catalonia.

Tracy Cogswell and Dan Whiteley were among the fifty-four. They had both had a bellyful of the Commie conduct of the war. Indebted to the Soviets for its munitions, planes, tanks, and artillery, the Spanish state had fallen under the control of Stalin's representatives from Moscow. And that had been the kiss of death.

By that time, Tracy and Dan Whiteley were the closest of friends.

Chapter Four

There came a knock at the door. Tracy got up and went over to it.

It was Betty. She smiled and said, "Lunch is on, Tracy." She couldn't have looked prettier, he thought.

The academician was already at the table, but Jo Edmonds was nowhere in sight when Betty and Tracy issued forth onto the terrace where meals were usually taken. Evidently, these people spent as much of their time in the sun as they could. The house was so constructed as to allow for that.

Tracy looked about and said, "Where's Jo?"

Walter Stein said, "Over in Gibraltar looking up a potential member of our organization."

"Your underground organization, eh?" Tracy took a chair. He was on familiar ground now. "Does the government give you much of a hard time? In my day, some countries tolerated the existence of the movement, but some cracked down hard, especially the dictatorships, ranging from Spain and Portugal to Russia and China. The United States was about halfway between. Theoretically, we were allowed to exist, but actually we got quite a bit of guff from the FBI and various Congressional committees about what they called un-American activities. How does your government stand?''

"What government?'' Stein said, helping himself from the casserole dish before them.

Tracy looked at him impatiently and said, "The government you're trying to overthrow. The state. You said you were an underground.''

"Oh.'' The other cleared his throat. "I used that term merely to clarify our position in your mind. There is no government any more.''

Tracy's impatient look had turned into a stare. "No government! You've got to have some sort of government! In our day, the organization looked forward to a time when there would be a minimum of government. There were some eleven million people working in the bureaucracy then, in the United States alone. It was probably worse in Russia. But you've got to have *some* government.''

Betty helped herself from the serving dishes. "Why?'' she said reasonably.

He was floored by her answer. "Why . . . why to operate things. Otherwise, you'd have chaos.''

The academician made a wry face. "We have an International Congress of Guilds which coordinates production, transportation, communications, distribution, medicine and so forth and so on, but it's a planning body, rather than a government, not to speak of a state. The name is a bit anachronistic, in view of the fact that we don't have nations any more.''

In irritation, Tracy shoveled up some food for himself. He had not eaten anything but superlative food since his awakening in this new world.

''Look,'' he said. ''Suppose I killed somebody. Deliberately. Cold-blooded murder, not an accident. What would happen to me? No cops, no courts, no jails?''

Stein said, ''Why, in case of such an antisocial act, the Medical Guild would take over and cure you.''

Tracy was sarcastic. ''Oh, great. So all crime is considered a medical matter, huh? That doesn't do the man who was killed any good.''

Betty sighed and said, ''Back in your day suppose you had an automobile accident. No one at fault, but several persons killed. Would you have done the dead victims any good for the authorities to jail or execute those who survived?''

''Well, sometimes they did jail them,'' Cogswell said.

''I don't see what is accomplished by punishing either a person who had an accident or a sick person.''

''I'll think about it some more and come back at you,'' Tracy said. He took another bite. ''Meanwhile, this is wonderful beef.'' He looked at Betty respectfully. ''Did you cook it?''

''Me?'' she said. ''Good heavens no. These dishes come from the automated community kitchens.''

''Automated!'' He looked down at his plate. ''You mean that you've automated even cooking? Admittedly, this food is superlative but cooking isn't one of the things you automate. It's . . . well, the conception is . . . terrible. I've eaten in what we used to call automats in my day. It's an attack on human dignity.''

Betty was surprised. ''Why? An autochef produces a dish perfectly every time it is ordered. It is impossible to burn it, oversalt or undersalt it, or make any other mistakes. Once the recipe is fed into the data banks it is there for all time. Every recipe of the cuisines of the world is included.''

He shook his head in frustration. ''Who is it that dreams up new recipes?''

''Anyone who wants to. Usually amateur chefs. It's crossfiled by type of dish, ingredients, region, if any, and——''

He interrupted sarcastically. ''Suppose I whomped up a recipe that involved a mixture of dill pickles, vanilla ice cream, chili peppers, mustard and chicken. Would they put that in the recipe banks?''

''Of course. Though it seems unlikely that anyone would ever order it . . . even you.''

''I give up,'' he said. ''At any rate, this is excellent beef. I don't recall much beef in this vicinity of Morocco in my day, and what there was was pretty grim. This tastes as though it must have come from Scotland, or at least the American Middle West.''

Stein chortled apologetically. ''Ah, I'm sorry about continually contradicting you, Tracy, but, you see, this beef was never grazed. In fact, it's stretching a point to call it beef. We no longer raise beef cattle. At least not in the old sense. It was very wasteful. The cow who originally supplied the bits of steak you are eating from the casserole probably lived some thirty or forty years ago."

Before Tracy could protest that nonsense, the academician hurried on. "In the same way that a Rembrandt can be duplicated, so can flesh, given the necessary ingredients on hand at the meat plants. It has a good many advantages, of course. Large areas of pasture land are unnecessary. And we don't reproduce portions of the animals such as hoofs, bones, or intestines; only those parts we desire. It also makes it impossible for the meat to be diseased, tough, or in other respects undesirable."

"I give up again," Tracy said. "And all this is automated, of course?"

"Of course."

Tracy took a few more bites before saying, "Listen, let's go back a ways. This, uh, underground of yours. Does it have much trouble agitating?"

Betty said, "Agitating?"

"Gettings its message across. Distributing its propaganda. Making speeches, infiltrating——"

"Oh," the academician said. "I see what you mean. No, certainly not. Not at all."

That set Tracy back a bit. He said, "You mean you can just go out and advocate overthrowing the present socioeconomic system and nobody says anything? No cops, nobody to shut you up?"

"We just told you that we no longer had government in the old sense of the word."

"But surely somebody is against you."

"Oh, yes," the other nodded. "And those who are against what we stand for write and speak against us."

Tracy Cogswell put his fork down and said patiently, "Who makes up your membership, who are your potential recruits, and who's against you?"

"Our potential recruits consist largely of those who still work, those who have the dream of continuing human advancement, those who wish to get the human race back on the track of advancement. Also organization material should be found among those who work on their own."

Tracy didn't realize that Stein hadn't answered part of his question. He scowled and said, "How do you mean, those who work on their own?"

Stein said, "Some, who are not selected by the computers, decide to work on their own as amateurs, I suppose you might call them. Especially scientists, artists, scholars——"

"Wait a minute. What do you mean, those not selected by the computers?"

"Why," the academician told him, "as I said earlier, there are very few positions to be occupied. Only the merest fraction of the population is needed to produce all we can consume. Many more apply for such positions as are available than are needed. Consequently, when there is an opening, the computers decide who is the person best suited for the job."

Tracy Cogswell, as usual these past few days, was at sea. He said, "Well, what's this amateur stuff?"

The other explained, saying, "Suppose, as in my

own case, I was particularly interested in medicine
. . . in my case, in some of the more esoteric fields of
medicine. The computers did not select me for any of
the few positions available in the field, so I continue my
researches on my own.''

Tracy said, ''And you have available all the materials, all the equipment, you need?''

''Yes, certainly.''

''Even though, actually, you are fighting against the,
whatever-you-called-it, the International Congress of
Guilds?''

Walter Stein frowned. ''I'm not exactly fighting
against the Congress, but even if I were, certainly I'd
have available any materials I wished. No one would be
in a position to forbid them to me.''

Tracy had given up eating any more. ''What do you
mean any materials? You mean you can get just anything you want? Suppose you wanted a king-size supply of opium. Do you mean that this distribution center
of yours would just deliver it to you, no questions
asked?''

''Why would I wish a large supply of opium?''

''How do I know?'' Tracy said impatiently. ''That
just came from the top of my head. But suppose.''

Betty said, ''You ask the strangest questions.'' She
too had finished her meal.

Stein said, ''Why, of course. Why. not?''

''Well, suppose you got hooked on it yourself and
also spread the stuff around so that Betty, here, and
Edmonds also got hooked?''

''You mean addicted?''

"Yes, I mean addicted."

"Then I imagine as soon as we had finished our investigations into opium addiction, we would consult the Medical Guild for a cure."

"Cure, eh?" Tracy said. "But suppose it was one of the really hard drugs, like heroin?"

"Oh, I see what you mean. Truly dangerous drugs. There are no drugs anymore, Tracy, that do not submit to cure. If one becomes addicted to a narcotic—and some have been developed artificially, much worse than the heroin of your day—he can be cured overnight. One aspect of the matters which the Medical Guild insists upon is a future, ah, allergy to the narcotic involved. That is, from the period when you became addicted and were then cured you can no longer take the drug again. That is, you could not become addicted again. Both your psyche and your physical body would reject it." He added, frowning, "There has been considerable debate upon this infringement upon your personal prerogative."

"Jesus Christ, I don't know how we get off on these sidetracks every time I start asking questions. We've gone from cooking to drug addiction by way of how to run an underground in the year 45 New Calendar. Getting back to this working on your own if the computers don't select you. Suppose you make a big breakthrough in some field. Some really offbeat thing like how to cure cancer."

"Oh, cancer was eliminated almost seventy-five years ago," the academician said.

"All right, all right. I was just using it as an example.

109

What happens if you hit on something really worthwhile?''

''Then it's put into the data banks and from then on the race utilizes it.''

''And how do the damn computers feel about that, after turning you down as someone who should have had a job?''

The other shrugged. ''I would imagine that in the future they might well consider using my abilities in that particular field.''

Tracy said, half-disgustedly, ''I don't seem to be getting anywhere in understanding this century and I don't think I will be getting anywhere until I fill in more background. I think I'll go on back to my Interlingua. Sometimes I get the feeling you people aren't getting through to me because you're using a language that is awkward to you. A hell of a lot of what you say doesn't make any sense at all. At least it doesn't to me.''

Stein looked distressed. ''I am sorry, Tracy. But you must realize almost a century spans our eras. How would you like to be in the position of discussing the science of your period, for instance, with an averagely well educated man of the 1850s, back even before the Civil War? As I recall, the telegraph was just coming in and the fastest and most efficient means of transportation was the wood-burning steam locomotive. In your day, man was already beginning to reach into space was he not?''

''The Russians had launched the Sputnik,'' Tracy said. ''Which reminds me of something. One of you said the other day that you had observatories and so forth on the moon. That Sputnik just went around and around in orbit going beep-beep. What's happened in the past century?''

Stein said, ''Well, very briefly, the United States launched a program to get a man onto the moon in a decade. Supposedly, it was a race with the Russians. Evidently, the Russians didn't know about the race, or didn't care. They continued their own space program at a slower, less expensive pace. Initially, they made the greatest progress. They put the first earth-born animal into space, a dog. They put the first man up, and later the first woman. They were the first to put more than one person at a time into orbit and made the first space walk. But then American technology, backed with billions upon billions of dollars, forged ahead and before 1970 they had landed the first crewed spaceship on Luna.''

Tracy was fascinated. ''And then what happened?''

The other tried to remember details. ''Why, they brought back some rocks and things after making various observations. And afterward there were several other moon trips. And they sent up a, uh, sky lab, I think they called it, manned by three men at a time and did some more serious observations; and there was even some cooperation with the Russians after a time but people were already losing interest.''

''Losing interest!'' Tracy blurted in surprise. ''In a thing like that?''

Stein answered. ''Once again, I must remind you that my thinking in terms of your times is as though you were thinking in terms of the nineteenth century, before the American Civil War. But the thing is that the United States was spending too much, so far as finances and resources were concerned. They had become imbroiled in a ridiculous war in Indochina and remained in it for too long, supposedly in an effort to contain communism. Tens of billions of dollars were expended shoring up a corrupt, reactionary government.''

''That mess was already beginning in my time,'' Tracy said.

''Yes, well, at the same time the arms race with the Soviet Union was taking place, and America was plowing the better part of a hundred billion a year into that. With the space program also consuming its billions, the economy began to falter. At any rate, to get back to the point, the people began to lose interest in space in view of more immediate problems.''

''But how do things stand now?''

''For all practical purposes, they've dragged to a halt,'' Betty said in disgust. ''To put it in the idiom of your time, nobody gives a damn.''

Tracy protested, ''But you said there were some observatories on the moon.''

''Ummm. Automated. Radio Interferometers. In other words, radio telescopes,'' she said. ''We also have various communications satellites, all automated. But nobody has gone up into space since I was a child.''

Stein said, ''Twenty years ago they built a spaceship to send a man out to Jupiter and orbit it. They had sent unmanned probes out to the various other planets long before, but this was to be manned.''

''And what happened?'' Tracy said.

"They couldn't find anyone who would go. The risks were rather high and even with nuclear propulsion the trip would have been a long one."

"Nobody to go?" Tracy said blankly.

"That is correct," the academician nodded. "We keep telling you, Tracy, that the human race is turning to mush. Gone are the days when a Hillary would climb Mount Everest. Gone are the days when a Thor Heyerdahl and his crew of adventurers would cross the Pacific on a balsa raft, or the Atlantic in a papyrus boat, just to see if it could be done. These days people get their second-hand thrills watching make-believe on the tri-di television or dreaming of exciting things. So, for twenty years the spaceship has sat."

Tracy took a deep breath. "Some Utopia," he said.

"Yes," Stein said, nodding again. "You are beginning to comprehend why we brought you to this era, Tracy."

"Like hell I am," Tracy said, coming to his feet. "These are your problems. Solve them. For me, thus far I largely like what I see, even though I don't understand much of it. And now I'm going back to take another crack at Interlingua."

Chapter Five

Tracy Cogswell was a plugger. He always had been. Since his teens he had driven himself. The nearest thing he could remember to a vacation was the three years he had spent in the Stalag, near Krems, on the Danube river in Austria: three years in a Nazi concentration camp. But even there he had read assiduously and attended the classes that the other prisoners had taught. He had even studied art, drawing away with more élan than talent.

Now he was plugging at learning Interlingua. He stuck to it until summoned for dinner.

Jo Edmonds had returned from Gibraltar but said nothing about the results of his trip.

The others were intrigued with questioning Tracy about the working of his organization back in the 1950s, but he was more interested in practicing his Interlingua. He already knew the grammar, which was as simple as Betty had said, and now he was trying to get the correct accent. He was increasing his vocabulary very quickly under the drug stimulation.

He was already making tentative plans for his immediate future. As soon as he had picked up enough of the language and some know-how on the workings of this new world, he planned to return to North America. All his life he had looked forward to really seeing the land of his birth. He wanted to see the Rockies, Yellowstone Park, Yosemite. He wanted to fish along the Florida coast, go down one of the fast-flowing rivers in a canoe, tramp through the Smokies. All his life he had wanted to do these things. When he'd had an idle hour, in the old days, he'd leafed through the travel books and brochures.

Cogswell the incorruptible, the dependable, the lifelong devoted organization man. Ha! His Utopia was here. He was going to enjoy it.

After dinner he went back to the study. By this time he was into Secondary Interlingua. Betty had been right. It was a scientific language. It worked. He could see the advantages. All languages in the past had been fouled-up messes, even the more beautiful ones like Spanish.

Look at Spanish. It went back to the days when the Basques, wherever the hell they came from, had dominated most of the Iberian peninsula. Possibly the Cro-Magnons, who had done the fabulously beautiful animal drawings in the caves at Altamira, had spoken a language which later became Basque. Then came the Celts and later the Carthaginians with their Semitic language, and the Greeks with their language, and then the Romans with Latin. Then the Vandals and later the Visigoths, with Germanic tongues, and the Moslems with Arabic and Berber. And the Jews had been the intellectual leaders of Spain for a millineum.

So what kind of a language did Spanish shape up to be? They called it one of the Romance languages, based on Latin. But Tracy had never seen a Spaniard who could understand, say, a Rumanian, who supposedly also spoke a Romance language.

It must have been twenty o'clock—he had already found that they used the twenty-four hour clock these days—when a knock came on the study door. A very gentle knock.

He guessed that it was Stein, fussing around about his health, and ready to order him to bed; but it wasn't.

It was Betty, and she was obviously freshly out of her bath. He had never seen her looking prettier. And, somewhat to his surprise, she was in a quite transparent negligee.

He had already become used to the fact that the modesty of his own period didn't much apply to the present. Several times he had seen Betty topless, her excellent breasts openly in view, and wearing a bikini bottom even more revealing than those on the beaches of France in the 1950s. Neither her father nor Edmonds had seemed to notice. Evidently, the sight of a women's breasts were no more stimulating these days than the sight of a man's had been to a woman in his own era.

From the first, he had thought Betty Stein much more than averagely attractive, but it hadn't occurred to him that he would ever see her in a negligee, nor had he thought of her as available sexually. Indeed, he hadn't thought of sex since he had been brought to this century. It wasn't a field in which he had been overly active, since he had spent his time fully employed in the movement, in prison, or in an army or partisan group where women were hard to come by . . . at least, women who were attractive. It wasn't that he didn't have normal sexual drives, but Tracy Cogswell simply hadn't very often had the opportunity to indulge in sex. Oh, he'd had his moments, sometimes shacked up with a girl active in the movement, but as a whole his life had been on the monkish side.

Now, Betty, with a wry smile, said, "It occurred to me that you might be . . . lonesome."

"Lonesome?" he said inanely. All of a sudden his mouth was dry.

He stepped back into the room, to allow her entry, and looked at her in blank surprise.

Her forehead wrinkled a bit and she said, "Why, yes. It occurred to me . . . well, you haven't met any other women at all save me and you must have . . ."

It was just one more of the curves that had been thrown at him these past few days. He couldn't believe what was transpiring. Surely she couldn't have come in here in this outfit—it was so transparent that he could make out her dark pubic hair, which he tried to keep his eyes from—with anything in mind except . . .

Her frown deepened. On her, a puzzled frown was no detriment to her features. She said, though her voice portrayed that she couldn't possibly believe it, "Perhaps you would rather I go to Jo and suggest . . ."

He looked at her blankly. "Do you mean that Jo is, uh, queer?"

"Queer?"

This was the damnedest conversation Tracy Cogswell could ever remember having had. Here he was, confronted with one of the most attractive women he had ever met, obviously dressed—or undressed—for him, and they were standing, facing each other, talking about . . . talking nonsense.

He said, "A homosexual."

She said brightly, "Oh, no. Jo is quite normal. He likes everything. Women, men, group sex. I'm sure he would enjoy spending the night with you, or us, if that's what you like."

Tracy closed his eyes in pain. He opened them again and said, his voice a bit thick now, "Look, let's go into the other room. And, uh, no. I'm not interested in Jo. I . . . I like girls."

He followed her into his bedroom.

She turned and smiled and her mouth had a slightly mocking quality. "It occurs to me that it has been almost a century since you have had a woman."

They stopped next to the bed. He said, his voice thicker still, "The same thought just came to me. But, well, what would your father say?"

She began helping him remove his clothes.

"My father?" She obviously didn't get it. "Do you mean . . . well, are you one of these fellows who likes older men?" She seemed disappointed in him.

He slipped out of the shorts he had been wearing. "No," he said quickly. Good God what a conversation. "I told you, I like girls. I meant, here I am in his house, and, well, a guest, I suppose you'd say, although I didn't ask to be brought here. At any rate, you're his daughter, and here I am in his house and . . .''

He was nude now and, in spite of the fact that he was almost middle-aged, slightly embarrassed.

She said in puzzlement, "This isn't his house."

"Let's get into bed," he said, not wanting to pursue that. "We can discuss it later."

She threw back the bed cover and made a flick of hand to extinguish the lights. He had already found out about that remote control of the lights.

She said, "Or would you rather leave the lights on?"

"Never mind," he said hoarsely. "Either way. Just come over here."

"Like this?"

"Yes, like this." He took her into his arms, finding her immediately to be everything he could have guessed.

"Goodness," she said with a giggle, which was one of the last sounds Tracy had ever expected from the lips of the well-possessed Betty Stein, "but you're . . . ardent."

He began pawing her. Pawing was the only term that applied. His hands were moist. Her body was exactly what he could have expected her body to be. She was an extremely attractive young woman in her late twenties, in perfect health, and perfect in physical condition. He had the horrible feeling that if he didn't watch himself, and it was becoming increasingly difficult, that he'd come to orgasm even before entering her.

She caressed him too, though not with the same immediacy. And, of course, they kissed. The mouth of

Betty Stein was especially well constructed for kissing.

Tracy Cogswell felt like an adolescent virgin.

She murmured, "Do you particularly like any of the usual perversions?"

"What!"

She murmured, "Isn't that the term you used in your day? You must realize that I studied English second-hand. That is, from the data banks through the autoteachers, and from books. I'm wobbly when it comes to idiom. I can't remember, for instance, if you said 'scram,' or 'get lost,' or 'go get screwed,' or 'fuck off' during the period when my father put you into hibernation."

Tracy was desperate with passion. He said, "Look, we'll talk about slang later. But, meanwhile, no, I'm not particularly up on the perversions."

She said, "Do you want me to slip out of this nightgown?"

"Yes."

She slipped out of the nightgown and he grabbed her again and she grabbed him again.

He said, apologetically, "Listen, I'm afraid I'm not going to be able to hold it very long the first time. I . . . well, like you said, it's been a long time."

"Oh, that's all right," she said cheerfully. "I expected as much."

Only moments later, she sighed and said, "Was that nice?"

"Nice isn't exactly the word."

"Oh, I told you I wasn't particularly up on your idiom. What would the word be?"

"It's not a matter of idiom," he told her weakly. "Once again, as you said, it's been a century, roughly."

"Yes, of course," she murmured. "You know, I've always particularly liked sex. Ever since I was fourteen and my sex instructor taught me the standard positions, I——"

"The *who?*" he said.

"My *sex* instructor," she said, and then, "Oh, let me see. They probably didn't teach practical sex in your time, did they? I've read quite a few of the old novels. Everybody had to learn by themselves and rely on their instincts . . . like animals."

"Wait a minute, now," Tracy said. "You mean that you have teachers who teach you sex when you get to be fourteen years old?"

"Oh, I was quite mature at fourteen," Betty said earnestly. "Father said he thought it quite all right for me to begin instruction. So I had my hymen surgically removed and——"

"Wait a minute now," Tracy said again. "You mean that your father okayed having, well, you having sexual intercourse with a . . . a sex instructor, at the age of fourteen?"

She said, her voice very reasonable, "Yes, of course. I had already been menstruating for well over a year, and I was beginning to think more and more about it and wanting to have sex, so he decided that I'd better go ahead."

"Sex instructor," Tracy said in amazement. He tried to make a joke. "At least that's one thing that's not automated in this age. Now, there's a job I might like to have."

She seemed a bit surprised. "Well, why not then? When you've acclimated yourself a bit more and are completely physically recovered—it's rather hard work—why not apply to the Sexual Education Department of the Medical Guild? There's always a shortage of instructors. It's not so bad with the women instructors, since a woman can handle a half dozen or more students concurrently, but most men are hard put to work with more than three girls at a time, particularly if they have a permanent or semipermanent relationship going on otherwise."

He wasn't sure he was getting all of this, or, at least, getting it correctly.

He said, "Look here. What kind of people apply for this kind of job?"

"Why, like any other job. Those who like the work. Those who are dedicated to it."

"Wouldn't anybody like that kind of work?" He was being sarcastic. However, he was also beginning to recover from his first and startling orgasm and becoming conscious of the curves of her body as she snuggled up to him.

She said, "Of course not. It's considered to be quite an unselfish contribution to society and is a highly honored field. What could be more necessary than the sexual education of youth? But it's a terrible drain on one. Can you imagine a girl volunteering and being mauled over, time and time again, by callow boys in their teens? And, for the first few weeks, and often months, they usually ejaculate prematurely and the poor instructor almost invariably is left dangling, aroused but unsatisfied. Oh, believe me, the sex instructor's job is no great treat.''

He said cautiously, ''I suppose that would apply to the women instructors . . . but the men, with all the teeny-boppers?''

''The what?''

''The young girls. Like you, when you were fourteen or so.''

She was surprised at what he had said. ''Goodness, what man in his right mind would want to bother with an inexperienced child when he could spent his nights with an experienced woman? By the way, darling, you're already growing firm again. This time. . . .''

Chapter Six

In the morning, when Betty and Tracy issued forth onto the terrace the two men were already there.

Betty had donned a pair of very brief shorts and wore nothing else, not even shoes. She looked sleepily satisfied, like a kitten that's just been into the cream. She had shown Tracy how to go about ordering from the Tangier distribution center. It seemed that deliveries were made through some sort of vacuum chute and arrived practically immediately, deposited in the delivery box.

Previously either the academician or Edmonds had brought clothing to Tracy. Now he was in a sport shirt and kilts, very suited to the climate. On his feet were a comfortable pair of sandals that didn't look as though they were of leather, though the material resembled it. They were obviously brand new but had no need to be broken in. Tracy wondered if they threw them away at the end of the day to be recycled.

At the appearance of the newcomers both of the men looked up, Stein somewhat startled. He said hurriedly,

"You haven't been overdoing, have you Tracy Cogswell?"

Tracy thought inwardly, "Jesus Christ, here I've just spent the whole night with his daughter and the only thing he thinks of is my health."

He said, "I'm fine."

Betty said, "Oh, father, stop worrying about him. He's as strong as a horse. I'll go get breakfast."

There was a slightly amused look on Jo Edmonds' easy-going face. He said to Betty. "Learn any new techniques?"

"No," she said flippantly over her shoulder. "Not yet, at least."

With a rather ridiculous twinge of jealousy, Tracy realized that Betty's bed was probably not an unknown to Jo Edmonds. He sat at the table and for a moment stared out over the straits.

He said, "You know, it occurs to me that I haven't seen a ship since I arrived. In my day there was hardly a time when you couldn't see at least a dozen in the straits at any given time. But it would seem to me that with all the increased production you'd have shipping all over the place."

The academician shook his head and smiled. "No. As a matter of fact, we don't have cargo ships any more. Oh, we've got pleasure ships, yachts, even windjammers, and luxury cruise ships for those who like travel on the sea, but no more cargo ships, and we have comparatively little transport across the oceans."

As usual, Tracy was staring at him. He said, "That simply does't make sense."

"Yes it does. You see, in your day most shipping was of bulk objects such as oil and coal and quite a bit of wheat and other cereals. But with nuclear fusion, very little of the fossil fuels are utilized anymore. And most cereals are raised near where they are consumed."

"But you have to have some intercontinental trade!" Tracy protested.

"Yes, certainly," the other said. "But we don't use ships, which were terribly inefficient. Suppose, for instance that a factory in your day in Switzerland wished to send some of its product to, say, Kansas City. It would put the product on a train and send it to a port on the Atlantic coast, where it would be unloaded and put on a ship. The ship would sail to New York and the product would be unloaded and placed on a train, or in trucks, and hauled to Kansas."

"So how do you do it now?"

"With hover cargo craft. It is loaded at the factory in what you used to call Switzerland and proceeds to the Atlantic and takes to the water. It crosses the ocean and emerges onto the land and goes on out to the middle west and unloads at its destination. All automated, of course."

"Of course," Tracy said. He shook his head and changed subjects. "One thing I've got to do is learn the everyday way of doing things. The way things are now, if I left this house I'd probably starve to death."

"I rather doubt it," Edmonds said. He brought his piece of jade from a pocket and began idly to thumb it.

Tracy looked at Stein. "For instance, Betty mentioned last night that you didn't own this house. But if there's no money how can you pay rent? Who does own it?"

"You misunderstood her," the academician told him. "I don't own the house but neither does anybody else."

Tracy thought he understood. He said, "You mean it's owned by the government?"

Jo Edmonds said mildly, "As we told you, there is no government in the sense of the word you're using it."

"Well," Tracy said, exasperated. "How did you get the house? How come you were allowed to move into it, instead of somebody else?"

The academician was patient. "We had it built. When we first came over here to the Tangier area from America, for the experiment on you, we checked with the local distribution service, selected a site near where we planned to have you interred and then later brought out of hibernation, and had the house built."

"And when you go back to America, what will you do with it?"

"Why, just leave it. If someone else wishes to move in—it's a superlatively attractive location, I think —they could but more likely it would be recycled."

"Recycled! A house this?" Tracy looked about him in utter disbelief. "See here, how long did it take to build it?"

"Two or three days." The other looked at Jo Edmonds. "Wasn't it?"

"A couple of days, as I recall," Edmonds answered idly, and then said to Tracy. "Houses these days are largely prefabricated, and the labor involved in assembling them is automated.''

Tracy couldn't believe it. ''So when you leave here to go back to your home in America, you just leave this place to be recycled?''

''We have no home in America,'' Stein said.

Tracy looked at him. ''Where did you live in America?''

''The last time, in the Catskill Mountains in what used to be the state of New York.''

''In a house, I assume.''

''Why yes. Some people prefer to live in apartments, but most choose houses. Ours was a somewhat smaller place than this, since it was before Jo came to live with us, and you, of course. So there were only Betty and me.''

Tracy said, ''So when you decided to come over here you just left it, and now it's probably been recycled?''

''Yes.''

Tracy couldn't get it. He said, ''But wouldn't you want a permanent place in which to store your things?''

''What things?'' the other said reasonably.

''Your private possessions. Your personal belongings.''

Betty had returned bearing a tray with breakfast. She sat it on the table.

She said, ''Tracy, you are very difficult to get through to. Hasn't it become obvious to you? We don't have any personal belongings.''

''I have a few books that I've marked up,'' the academician said.

Jo Edmonds said, after laughing a little, "And I have this."

Tracy Cogswell stared at him. "You mean to tell me that in this whole world you own nothing whatsoever except that silly piece of stone?"

"That's right. And a few other pieces."

Tracy turned to Betty in absolute disbelief. "But you, surely you must have some favorite clothes, things like that, which you treasure."

She said, "Of course I have favorite clothes. And every time I want to wear them, I simply dial the distribution center and they send them over. Brand new, obviously."

He said desperately, "But little personal things, like possibly photographs of your mother, or friends when you were a kid."

"If I wanted to see a picture of my mother . . ."

"I know . . . I know. You dial the data banks and all the pictures of your mother ever taken are on file."

He couldn't think of anything else to say. Of all the things that had come up in this crazy world of the future thus far, this probably flabbergasted him more than anything else. He took a deep gulp of his coffee before trying again.

"How about your car?" he said. "The hover-car or whatever you call it, that you took me over to Spain in. When you leave here certainly you aren't going to just leave it to be recycled or whatever."

"It's not our car," Betty said. "When we came here we applied for a car. Since we live way out here on the cape, we keep it on a full-time basis, rather than summoning a different one from the car pool each time we need it. When we leave, we'll return it to the car pool. If it's still in good shape, they'll continue to use it. If not, it will be recycled. Nobody owns cars anymore, Tracy. Who'd want to own a car?''

"Everybody did, in my day," he said.

"Yes," she said. "And there were so many of them that the country was overflowing. These days we order a car only when we have need for one. In that way, you can order exactly what you need, a little sports run-about, a limousine if several of you are making a trip, a camper if you wish to go camping, a heavy-duty vehicle if you're making a trip up into the mountains or out into the desert where there are few facilities.''

Academician Stein had been thinking it over. He said, "I think that what you should attempt, Tracy Cogswell, is to conceive of the present differences in our outlook on the ownership of *things*. In your time, practically everyone strove to amass as much property as he could. It was both the symbol and reality of success. People lived in as large a house as they could manage, usually regardless of their needs. I have read of British country estates which had literally hundreds of servants. To what end? So numerous were the servants that servants had to be hired to take care of their needs and eventually servants to take care of the servants who took care of the servants. After a time it becomes ridiculous. The owner of the estate undoubtedly didn't even know the names of more than a score or so of his servants.

''But it didn't simply apply to homes. Everybody

wanted a larger car and more of them. It was an status symbol to have two, three, four or more cars, and possibly a private airplane, or even a yacht, as well. On top of all these possessions, each person accumulated as much clothing as possible, storing it about the house.''

Tracy said, ''I've got you now. Your paintings. You have some beautiful paintings, statuary, and other art objects all over the house. Don't tell me that you're going to just ditch them when you leave.''

''Why not?'' Betty said wonderingly. ''When we get back to America, if that's where we go to live next, we'll just order a new selection.''

Tracy Cogswell closed his eyes momentarily in a silent plea to the gods. He said, ''I'd forgotten about your duplicators. It's almost impossible for me to conceive of the absolute waste of this period. The drain on natural resources must be terrible.''

''What waste?'' Edmonds said. ''Practically everything we use that can be recycled, we recycle. With nuclear fusion, power is all but free. With unlimited power you can tap the resources of the sea. As has been pointed out, one cubic mile of sea water contains some one hundred and fifty million tons of solid material, including about twenty tons of gold, eighteen million tons of magnesium and just about all of the other elements in quantity. Given infinite power, they can be extracted. Or take a hundred tons of plain igneous rock such as granite. It contains on an average, eight tons of aluminum, five of iron, twelve hundred pounds of titanium, one hundred and eighty pounds of mag-

131

nesium, seventy of chromium, forty of nickel, twenty of copper, four of lead, ten of tungsten and many others. What natural resources did you think we were running out of, Tracy?''

For some reason, Tracy was irritated with them once again. Their answers were all so damned pat. Perhaps it was because they made him appear like a fool.

''Okay,'' he said. ''If the world is so affluent now, if you've got so damn much of everything, why aren't you happy? The picture you've been drawing for me is that the world is going to pot, then you turn around and tell me everybody has everything they want.''

Stein smiled sadly. ''Perhaps that's it, Tracy. Perhaps we don't want everything we want.''

''That obviously doesn't make any sense at all, damn it,'' Tracy snapped.

''Perhaps it does,'' the other said. ''There is no such thing as happiness, Tracy. Or, at least, only for very short periods of time. There is only the pursuit of happiness, as they put it in the Declaration of Independence. Whoever wrote that—and it has been debated whether it was Tom Paine, rather than Thomas Jefferson, though he has been given the credit—knew of what he spoke. Man pursues happiness, he doesn't achieve it. Have you ever met anyone of whom you could say, 'there is a happy man?' Can you point out a single example in all of history of which you could say, 'there was a happy nation?' The Greeks, the Cretans, the Mayans, the Peruvians under the Incas? No. There has never been a happy nation, and I rather doubt that there ever will be one.''

''This is getting a little far out for me,'' Tracy said,

finishing his coffee. "What have we been fighting for, down through the ages, if it wasn't for happiness? No matter how square that might sound."

"Man has been *pursuing* happiness. Like your branding of this society Utopia; it is a goal never attained. It can never be attained. Happiness is a contrast, not a permanent reality. No mentally balanced human being has ever attained permanent happiness. He can't because it is a contrast. It's like pleasure and pain. You must have them both, in their time. Some individuals obtain more than the average of one, and less of the other, but for all of us there must be both. That's why the conception of heaven and hell are invalid. Suppose, under the beliefs of some of the primitive religions I was consigned to either paradise or hell. Can you imagine perpetual pleasure . . . for all eternity? I suspect it would become quite boring after the first few thousand years. Or can you picture perpetual pain? Suppose they threw me into that lake of boiling sulphur, or whatever it was that Dante portrayed in his Inferno. Do you think it would bother me after the first five thousand years?"

"As I said," Tracy protested, "this gets a little far out for me. I'm a simple soul. The breakfast was excellent, Betty. Thanks."

"No thanks to me," she said, beginning to put the remnants on the tray. "And tomorrow I'll show you how to do the ordering and you can take your turn at it, my fine feathered friend."

He looked at her quickly. "You mean that everybody shares in . . . well, whatever housework has to be done and that I've been freeloading?"

All three of them laughed at him.

Stein said, "There's precious little that has to be done, these days, Tracy, but yes, everyone in a household shares. Didn't you have something called women's lib in your days? Well women have been 'libbed.' "

Tracy shook his head. "It must have come later. I've never heard of it."

Jo Edmonds said cooly, "You seem to be up to just about anything by now. How about a night on the town, after you've finished your studies today?"

Chapter Seven

Tracy spent the day on his Interlingua, taking stimmy after stimmy. He had gotten to the point now where all he needed was vocabulary. Even correct accent and pronounciation had been quite easily acquired, since the rules were so few and so obvious. There was no such thing as having three words—*lea, lee,* and *leigh,* for example—all meaning something different, and being pronounced exactly the same. There was no such thing as having pliers, trousers, and scissors, all supposedly plural when there is no singular pliar, trouser, or scissor.

No, he was taking to Interlingua like a whirling dervish in a revolving door. He took time out only for lunch and hurried through that. During it, he had just one major argument in the continuing debate with the other three about the workings of this present-day society.

He said to Stein, ''At breakfast you mentioned that in my day everyone wanted to accumulate property, privately owned possessions. Okay, and you say these days nobody cares a damn about owning things. But there must be exceptions. That rich man you mentioned, that owned a private airplane and even a yacht. Suppose I wanted a yacht these days? Everything is free, so I'd get it, eh?"

The other was puzzled. "Why not? But what would you do with it?"

"What do you think I'd do with a yacht? Obviously, I'd sail in it."

Edmonds said, "It would have to be a rather small yacht, if you just wanted it for yourself. Otherwise, who would crew it for you?"

Tracy looked at him in frustration.

Betty said, "A good many people like yachting. They usually join a yachting club and share the work involved. Or several compatible people will team together and operate one. In the old days the men that crewed a big yacht were the servants of the owner. We don't have servants any more."

He didn't give up, quite yet. "Okay. That private airplane deal. Today, I could just order one and keep it as long as I wanted, eh?"

"Certainly," Stein said.

"All right. Suppose it develops a knock in the engine, or whatever, and I have to take it into an airport to have it worked on. If practically nobody works, who'd repair my engine?"

Edmonds said, "It would probably be pulled, with automated equipment, and a new engine inserted and . . ."

"I know, I know. And the old one recycled. But

suppose it was something besides the engine, some-thing that just couldn't be replaced automatically?''

The academician said, ''If the aircraft was in such bad shape as all that, they would probably recycle the whole thing and give you a new one. You see, Tracy, we very seldom repair things anymore. With the com-puters, with automation, with unlimited power and with unlimited raw materials, we find it easier to build a new object rather than repair an old one.''

''Jesus Christ,'' Tracy said, tossing his napkin to the table and coming to his feet. ''I'm going on back to my · Interlingua. As soon as I get it really down pat, I'm going to take a course in historic developments between the years 1955 Old Calendar and 45 New Calendar.''

''A very good idea,'' Stein nodded approvingly.

As Tracy left, Jo Edmonds called after him, ''Don't forget our night on the town.''

He hadn't forgotten, although he had wondered what the other had in mind, and how it fitted into the scheme of things. He doubted very much if the younger man would have made such a suggestion unless he was up to something. Whatever it was, Betty and her father were probably in on it, since they had nothing to say.

After dinner the two of them strolled out to the garage and got into the hover-sedan which Betty had utilized to show him Gibraltar and the Costa del Sol.

Edmonds took the driver's seat and Tracy sat next to him. He'd have to learn how to drive one of these fancy crafts, he decided. When he was on his own, it would be a necessity.

However, Edmonds muttered, his voice lazy, ''The

AFTER UTOPIA

hell with driving manually," and began fiddling with a dial set into the dashboard.

This was a world of goddamned dials, Tracy Cogswell decided.

The craft took off after emerging the few feet out of the garage. There were no hands on the wheel, and Tracy was horrified, especially now that they were airborne, and at one hell of a clip.

He cried out, "For holy Jesus Christ's sake, what are you doing?"

Edmonds was unperturbed. "I hate driving, so I dialed our destination."

"Jesus," Tracy repeated. "You mean even this thing's automated?"

The other was puzzled and said, "Yes, of course. Didn't you already have some automated traffic in your time? I thought you did."

"No," Tracy said grimly, "and it makes me nervous. Where are we going on this big night on the town?"

"Torremolinos," Edmonds said. "There it is, up ahead. Terrible place, don't you know?"

Tracy could see the lights up ahead. He said, "I had got the impression that most people didn't live in cities."

"There are no more cities. Who would want to live in one? Dirty, crowded, terrible air . . ."

Tracy said wryly, "When you people grabbed me, the whole damn population of the world was graviating toward the cities. It was one of the big problems; they were getting too big to function."

138

"Economic necessity, not love of city life," Edmonds said. "They had to go for jobs, when the small farms folded up. Or for business reasons . . . or to get on relief. We don't have any of those motivations any more."

"And you say this isn't Utopia," Tracy muttered under his breath. He stared down at the beach and sea below them. "Listen," he said. "What keeps this thing up?"

"You mean the car?"

"Obviously, I mean the car."

Edmonds shrugged lazily. "I haven't the vaguest idea. It's not my line." He thought about it. "I've don't believe I've ever met anybody whose line it was. Of course, the computers do most of the designing of vehicles these days."

"You mean computers can devise new inventions?"

"Why, yes. With some supervision by highly advanced specialists." Jo Edmonds thought about it. "At least I think they are still supervised a bit. It's not really my line."

For some reason or other, Edmonds still occasionally exasperated Tracy. He said now, his voice almost a snarl, "Just what in the hell *is* your line, Edmonds? How do you fit into all this?"

"How do you mean?"

"I mean, who in the hell are you? How do you fit in? Old Man Stein is the crackpot scientist who brought me through to this century. Betty is his daughter, who seems to double as a nurse, or whatever. But where do you fit in?"

139

"Oh," Edmonds said. "I see what you mean, I should think." He'd brought out his piece of flat jade and flicked it. "It would seem that I'm the Tracy Cogswell of this century." He made an amused grimace.

"You're what!"

"I'm the nearest thing to your counterpart, Cogswell. I'm the organization's trouble-shooter. I'm the tough guy. I do the leg work. The organization sends me in when the situation calls for, uh, movement."

Tracy was amazed. "You!"

"That's right," Edmonds said softly. "We have to utilize what small resources we have. Now do you begin to see why we brought you from the past?"

"Tough guy! Why, for Christ's sake . . ."

"Yes. However, do not carry it too far. I have made my bones, Cogswell."

"Made your bones! Are you all the way around the bend? You can't know what that means. That's an old Mafia term. It means killing your first man."

"Yes, I know."

But you told me that if somebody killed somebody else the Medical Guild took over. They did something so that you'd never do it again."

"That's correct."

"And I got the impression that if you pulled some trick like that you just kind of turned yourself in and they . . . took care of you."

"Yes, that is correct. That is the usual thing."

"But you didn't turn yourself in?"

"No," Edmonds admitted. "You see, old chap, I

140

was of the opinion that possibly the organization might need me again . . . in the same eventuality.''

"Oh, brother. You people get farther out by the minute. What did you hit this guy for?''

"I beg your pardon?''

Tracy said impatiently, "This man you shot. Why did you have to do it?''

"I see. Well, in actuality he was a very strong critic of the ideas we were trying to put over. He thought it quite insane that we should wish to change present-day society.''

"That makes two of us,'' Tracy said. "So do I. This society has it made, from everything I've seen so far.''

Edmonds said, "He went to the extreme of wishing to initiate a return to laws, at least to the extent of outlawing our organization. He was a very aggressive man, very violent. I went to remonstrate with him.''

"I love that term remonstrate,'' Tracy muttered. "I too, in my time, have been sent to remonstrate with people. Mussolini for one. I was working with a group of partisans up near Lake Como and he was trying to escape over the line to Switzerland with what remained of the fascist gold supply. We remonstrated with him. It was one of the most satisfying sights I've ever seen, him dangling by his heels in that gas station.'' Tracy paused, in reflection. "Always felt sorry for the girl, Clara, though. She just wasn't important. Just a whore. Tony shouldn't have shot her. We shot people easy, though, in those days.''

Edmonds looked at him from the side of his eyes, seemingly surprised. "Mussolini! Did you actually meet him? To us, he is history. It's as though you met someone who knew Napoleon. But I thought the men who executed him were Communists. You weren't a Communist.''

It seemed a very long time ago . . . and it was. Tracy said, ''Yeah, I met the bastard, in passing, just before we shot him. No, I wasn't a Communist. At the time I was working with the American OSS, an outfit that I hated, but the thing was, what I wanted most was to hit characters like Mussolini, Hitler, Franco. I wouldn't have minded taking a crack at Stalin, either, but you can't have everything.''

''Hit?'' Edmonds said.

Tracy snorted at him. ''You're not as up on Mafia jargon as you'd like to think. It means to kill. You say you've made your bones. Okay, I have, in my time, God forgive me, hit more men than you have years to your life.'' He took a deep breath before saying, ''Some of them shouldn't have been killed.''

He got back to the present. ''At any rate, what happened to your boy?''

Edmonds said carefully and distastefully, ''He took violent exception to me and attempted to kill me. So I had to shoot him.''

''Shoot him?'' Tracy said, surprised. ''So you people still have guns kicking around here in Utopia.''

Edmonds said, ''There are not many. But there is still some hunting, and some weapons carried by game preserves officers, explorers, and so forth.''

''Explorers!''

The other accepted his surprise. ''We have deliberately kept some parts of the planet as they were originally. Borneo and the Amazon, for instance. It is invaluable for students in a score of subjects, including anthropology. We've even restored some areas to what they were in the past. Montana and North Dakota, as you called them in your time. Buffalo and other wildlife now have free range there. And there are still such things as poisonous snakes, wild boar, that sort of thing. So, yes, it is still possible to procure firearms. But here we are at Torremolinos.''

The vehicle was descending rapidly. Edmonds took over the manual controls, to Tracy's relief. There was a large building below them, with a parking area around it. It wasn't particularly well lit.

Tracy could barely identify the town of Torremolinos. He had been there on several occasions in the distant past—clandestinely, since the organization hadn't been popular with the Franco *Guardia Civil*. But in those days it had been a rather small fishing village and art colony. It was beginning to attract the tourist hordes when Academician Stein had grabbed his mind, but even then it was nothing like this.

He could recognize a few landmarks. The Torremolinos tower—going back to Moorish days, so he understood—was still there, out overlooking the sea. The beach was the same, three or more miles of it. Certain coves, he could recognize. But not even the central plaza remained in the town proper. There were no buildings more than two stories high, and in general everything was spread over a much wider area. As Edmonds had said, it would seem that people didn't

143

like to live in cities any more, nor even what used to be thought of as towns. Torremolinos was spread over a large area.

Tracy said, "If there aren't any cities anymore, what would you call this place?"

They had touched down, or, at least, hovered just a few inches from the ground. Edmonds was pulling up closer to the building. It was a pleasant enough structure, covering possibly an acre of land, and it seemed to be at least half sunken in the ground. The top was largely a garden, that even had trees.

"Torremolinos? It's a Pleasure Center. A resort, I suppose you'd say."

"I see," Tracy said. "And what's this particular building, a night club?"

They had come to a halt. Edmonds touched a stud and the vehicle settled to the tarmac of the parking area.

He said, "Not exactly. It's a narcotic center."

"Narcotic center? How do you mean?"

Edmonds explained. "A good many people like to take their narcotics in company. Some don't. They'd rather take them in privacy, but many like congenial company. Usually it's according to what drug they're on. This is a place where you can smoke, take your pills or injections, and enjoy whatever narcotic it is that you appreciate."

Tracy said, "You mean that we could, say, just walk in and order a pipe of opium, or, say a hypo of heroin, and sit around with like-mind' folk and blow our minds?"

The other said, "The opiates are passé. I doubt if any would be immediately on hand, though it shouldn't take too long to synthesize some of you were interested in experimenting with the older narcotics.''

"Such drugs as morphine are no longer used? Even for medicinal reasons?'' That set Tracy back.

Edmonds frowned, as though trying to remember. "I thought the opiates, all of them, were being phased out even in your time."

"Well, they weren't," Tracy told him. "Heroin, for instance, was one of the biggest problems in America."

"Ummm. Well, at any rate, drugs based on plants such as the opium poppy, the coca of Peru, or the so-called sacred mushroom *Psilocybe* have long since been replaced by laboratory-produced drugs. They are much more effective, either for medicine or . . . pleasure."

"And addiction can be cured immediately?"

"Just about."

The other began to open the door on his side.

Tracy said, "Just a minute. What in the world did you have in mind?"

"I thought that we'd go in, and you might want to give something a try."

"Well, think again," Tracy told him definitely. "I have no intention of blowing my brains out with some drug I've never even heard of before. The furthest I ever went in that direction was smoking kif once or twice."

"Kif?"

"That's what they called it in Morocco. Marijuana, bhang, pot, weed . . . Indian hemp."

"Oh," Edmonds said. "You mean cannabis. Few

ever resort to it these days, anymore than they do tobacco. Hard on the health. But there are other narcotics that might intrigue you, Cogswell.''

''No thanks. Alcohol is far enough along the line for me,'' Tracy said.

The other started up the car again. ''Very well, there's a nightclub overlooking the sea. Very attractive. Well go there.''

As they drove, Tracy looked over at his companion and said, ''Have you ever tried any of these new narcotics?''

''A few times,'' Edmonds said easily. ''They don't appeal to me. But I've tried everything . . . twice. Here we are.''

The building they drew up before was quite similar to the one they had just left, save that it was located on a cliff with a beautiful view up and down the coast. They parked and entered.

It wasn't as different as all that from some of the night spots of his own era, Tracy thought, with the exception that there were no waiters or bartenders, though there was a lengthy bar, complete with stools. all was automated, Tracy realized. Wasn't there anything in the way of work that couldn't be automated?

The table they took was inset with a lengthy wine list and there was a dial. There was also a phone screen.

Edmonds said, ''What'll you have, Tracy?'' It was the first time he had called the traveler from the past by his first name.

''What do you recommend . . . Jo?''

''Personally, I'm rather keen on a slightly sparkling Riesling wine.''

146

Tracy Cogswell had had in mind something stronger, but he shrugged and said, "Let's give it a try."

Each name on the wine list had a number next to it. Edmonds dialed. Within moments, the table's center sunk and then returned with a chilled bottle and two glasses. The bottle was of the type Tracy associated with the Rhine river—green, tall, and slim.

Edmonds poured.

The wine was certainly as good as any Tracy had ever tasted, clean and fruity. He said, "I don't see how in the devil you could automate a vineyard."

"Oh, this isn't made of grapes, you know. It's produced in automated factories. We can turn out much more acceptable wines now than were ever made from grapes."

"I give up," Tracy muttered. He turned to look about the night spot. In the best tradition, the lights were low and there was music, faint music, coming from somewhere. The place held at least a hundred tables, and was fairly well packed. They had been lucky to get a table.

There wasn't any dance floor, which somewhat surprised Tracy, particularly in view of the fact that the clientele was quite young. Another thing that surprised him was that, although obviously the drinks on the tables were in wide variety, including spirits and cocktails, nobody seemed much under the influence of the booze.

The screen on the table lit up. Jo Edmonds said something into it and then, to Tracy, "It's for you."

"For me? How could it possibly be? I wouldn't know anyone here." He looked at the screen. In it was a sparkling, vivacious redhead with bright green eyes. She was about twenty.

She smiled pertly and said, "Would you two like to join in with a six-way? Nothing goes but fellatio and cunnilingus." She spoke in Interlingua but the last two words were the same as in English.

Chapter Eight

Tracy gaped at her.

Jo Edmonds leaned over and said to her, "Not just for the moment, but thanks, dear."

She looked disappointed but smiled her pert smile again and faded off.

Tracy turned to his companion. "What the hell kind of a place is this, a whorehouse? And what did she mean, a six-way?"

"There is no prostitution any more," Edmonds said mildly. "This is a group-sex center. You take a table and then look about the room. If you see someone that appeals to you, the way you evidently appealed to the redhead, you phone her, or him, and discuss what you have in mind. You keep on phoning around until you've got your group organized. There are rooms upstairs."

"Group sex?"

"Yes. Anywhere from three persons up."

"Jesus," Tracy said. "Look, suppose I didn't want to work out with five other people, or up, but would like to go to bed with, say, the redhead who just phoned us?"

Edmonds said reasonably, "Then why come to a group-sex center? You can pick up a single girl in any establishment, or out on the street for that matter. Would you like to go upstairs and watch?"

"Watch what?"

Edmonds explained. "Some of the groups don't mind being watched while they perform. In fact, some of them like to be. Exhibitionists, you know. They're in rooms that have large windows, usually with one way glass, so that you can look in and watch, but they can't see out."

"A voyeur's dream world, eh?" Tracy said in disgust. "No thanks. For me, sex has always been a personal thing. I don't want any group action and I don't want to watch someone else getting their gun. Let's get ut of here. I'm beginning to get a bad taste in my mouth."

Jo Edmonds finished his glass of wine and stood. "Why not, old chap," he said, leading the way toward the door.

When they got back into the car, Tracy said sourly, "Some night on the town. What's next?"

"Well, let me see," Edmonds said as though considering alternatives. "There's another club over here devoted to sadists and masochists. If you'd be interested, we could . . ."

"You've got to be joking."

"No, not at all."

"You mean it's openly allowed?"

"Who could say no? They are consenting adults. Most who attend the place have fairly mild cases. They like to whip or be whipped, usually. Some like to be beaten up a bit, or to beat somebody else up. Actually, there is a touch of sadism in most of us, though we try to restrain it. And quite a bit of masochism in some. So, at any rate, if you like to whip people, or be whipped, we could go on over."

"Now, just a minute," Tracy protested. "Suppose you whipped somebody to death?"

Edmonds thought about it. He hadn't started up the car as yet. He said, "I've never heard of such a case, though I'm not particularly up on the subject. It doesn't seem to me that a masochist would be so to the extreme of wanting to be killed. And I rather doubt that many normal sadists wish to go to the point of killing even a consenting adult."

"Normal sadists," Tracy said indignantly. "How in the hell can you be a normal sadist?"

Edmonds looked at him, a twirk of humor on his easygoing face. He said, "Tracy, when indulging in preintercourse sex play, have you ever spanked a girl on her buttocks?"

Tracy scowled at him for a long moment. Finally, he said, "Yes, but she didn't object. I think she rather liked it. It was just for fun."

Edmonds laughed at him. "A couple of amateur sadists and masochists."

"That wasn't it at all, damn it!"

"Yes it was. You got a kick out of spanking her, and she got a kick out of being spanked. It probably brought on a quicker erection for you and prepared her for the act. Let's take another example. Did you ever beat a man insensible with your fists, or by kicking him, or whatever?''

Tracy froze. ''Yes.''

''Did you enjoy doing so?''

''Yes,'' Tracy had to admit. ''To the ultimate. He had just killed a very good friend of mine. He was a Moroccan soldier of Franco's, a son of a bitch of a mercenary who had just killed Bud Whiteley, who was basically one of the most gentle persons I have ever met. I hit the bastard's gun arm with an entrenching tool, disarming him. And then I went to work on him. When he was finally down, I kicked him in the side of the head. I hope the hell it killed him.''

''Very well,'' the other nodded, ''but you've just admitted that there can be pleasure in inflicting pain. Let's take the other side of the coin. Did you ever do any boxing, that is, the sport of pugilism?''

''Yes, as a matter of fact I have. In military training. What's that got to do with it?''

''When you were boxing, did you take pleasure in taking as well as receiving? That is, you took a blow, he took a blow, and on and on until one of you won. But the whole match . . . was it fun?''

''I see what you mean,'' Tracy admitted. ''Yeah, I enjoyed the whole thing, both giving and taking, no matter who won, though, of course, I preferred to win. In fact, I preferred to give the other guy more than I took.''

"A primitive sport," Edmonds said, starting up the car. "Today, in some places, they perform it as the Romans once did."

"How do you mean?"

"They wear, ah, I think the term you used in your day was brass knucks."

"Are you crazy?"

"No," Edmonds said, as though it was the most reasonable thing in the world. "They are consenting adults. If they wish to do that to each other, who is to say them nay? And if others enjoy watching the spectacle, who is to say them nay?"

The car was moving upward now.

Tracy said desperately, "To go back a ways. Suppose one of your sadists killed one of the masochists. What would happen?"

"I would imagine that the psychiatrists of the Medical Guild would treat him."

"Good God," Tracy muttered.

"I would think so," the other said judiciously. "It's not my field, but it would seem that such a person had gone somewhat beyond normality and should be treated."

Tracy Cogswell let his mind reel a moment or so at that before saying, "Where are we going now?"

"Well, how would you like to kill something?"

"How do you mean?"

Edmonds said, "How would you like to kill a dinosaur, or, say, a mammoth or a wooly mastadon? Did you hunt back in your own era?"

It seemed to Tracy that every time he got into a conversation in this age he wound up staring at the person he was talking to.

He said. "When I was younger I used to hunt rabbits and squirrels. I went out after deer a couple of times but had no luck. However, I always ate what I killed. My family could use meat. I didn't just kill——"

"It's different now," Edmonds interrupted him. "We seldom, if ever, eat . . . natural meat, I suppose you'd call it. However, if you would like to shoot a dinosaur, just for the, ah, hell of it——"

"You mean you've got some sort of king-size shooting gallery, or whatever, where you can pot away at a mechanical monster or——"

"No," the other man was shaking his head negatively. "I mean a real dinosaur, or, at least, as real as the biologists can reconstruct them."

"Nonsense."

"I beg your pardon?" Edmonds was driving manually now, and they were passing, from time to time, what seemed to be villas, sometimes restaurants, and, once, what looked like an amusement park of Tracy's time. The whole area seemed to be something like a more sophisticated Disneyland.

Tracy said flatly, "There is no such thing as a dinosaur. That was an animal that became extinct a million years before man ever came on the scene."

"Oh, you'd be surprised, I shouldn't think. Though in actuality man has been changing the animal world about him for a long time. Take the dog. Both the Pekingese and the Mastiff are of the same species and

154

can crossbreed. One was deliberately bred small, one large. Or the horse. The Shetland pony and the Percheron can crossbreed, or the horse and donkey, for that matter.''

"Listen,'' Tracy snorted, "it's a far cry from crossing a horse and donkey and getting a mule, to whomping up a dinosaur.''

"Yes. I was but using an example of man's interfering in genetics. But you must realize that during the knowledge explosion, which has slowed down considerably but is still going on, as many breakthroughs were made in the biological fields, including genetics, as in any others. Today, the scientists, computer aided, can create just about any life form that makes sense . . . and some that don't.''

Tracy was disgusted. "You're telling me that these scientists haven't anything better to do with their time than to recreate dinosaurs so that jaded thrill-seekers can shoot them?''

"Oh, it was originally done some time ago. I doubt if anybody is working on it anymore. But the information, the knww-how, is now in the data banks and if there is any call for a dinosaur they are raised, over in the Sahara, I believe, and——''

"In the Sahara! How could you raise anything in the worst desert in the world? Particularly something with as king-sized an appetite as a dinosaur would have.''

Edmonds seemed surprised that Tracy didn't know. "Oh, the Sahara has been almost completely reforested, Tracy. With nuclear power, it became practical to desalinate ocean water and pump it into the world's deserts. And, at the same time, the break-throughs in forestry enable us to force-grow some new species of trees as fast as flowers.''

"Holy smokes.''

"Yes. At any rate, would you like the experience of shooting a mammoth or a dinosaur? Actually, it's a rather boring proposition, don't you know? They're rather sluggish creatures and just stand there while you bang away at them with elephant guns.''

"No thanks,'' Tracy said sourly. "As I told you, I never hunted except when I ate what I killed. And I'll be damned if I want to eat a dinosaur; they're over-grown lizards aren't they? This is really some night on the town, all right. What comes next? What else has modern man dreamed up in the way of entertainment?''

Edmonds grinned lazily at him, even as they pulled up before a complex of four largely similar buildings. "This, I think you'll go for.'' But then he scowled. "Damn. Since I was over here last, they've added another building. That's bad. It would seem, I should think, that the, uh, entertainment is continuing to catch on.''

"What entertainment?'' Tracy said. Quite a few people were streaming in and out of the buildings, adults of all ages.

"These are Dream Palaces.''

Tracy looked at him, waiting for him to go on.

"Programmed dreams,'' the other explained. "Although that term doesn't quite explain it all. They aren't really all completely programmed, unless that's the way you want it, not using any of your own imagination. Actually——''

156

"What in the name of whatever is a programmed dream?"

"Well," Edmonds answered hesitantly, "in actuality they aren't dreams. Not in the usual sense. But, yes, I should think they are. It's just that they're artificially conceived, rather than haphazard, as ordinary dreams are."

Tracy sighed deeply, "Damn it, you're making less sense by the minute."

Edmonds scowled as he sought words to explain. "Really, what you get is artificial memories. They are composed, taped, and then fed into your brain. It's the most efficient of all forms of vicarious experience, often seeming more real than reality. You see, if you see a film, or tri-di show, a fictional story, you are living, vicariously, what the actors are going through. But in actuality, obviously, it isn't happening to you and all the time you realize it. Back in the old days when the Romans went to the arenas to watch gladiators kill animals or each other, the Romans watching were vicariously doing the killing. In the days when bull-fighting was at the height of its popularity in Spain and the Latin American——"

"Look, this gets wilder by the minute. What kind of dream do they have on tap?"

Edmonds grinned at him again, his lazy, insolent grin. "Just about everything. And if it's not on tap, as you say, they'll do it up for you. But, by this time, they've got just about everything available that you could desire. The adventurous type can request a dream in which he is a gunslinger out in the Old West of America . . . an Old West, which, I understand, never

157

really existed. In the dream, he fights Indians, shoots badmen, robs a stagecoach, rustles cattle, or whatever. And while it's going on it is so realistic that seemingly it is truly happening.''

"And what happens when he wakes up?''

"He retains the artificial memory as though it had truly happened.''

"What other kind of dreams, besides being Buffalo Bill, or Wild Bill Hickok?''

"You can imagine,'' Edmonds smiled, somewhat condescendingly. "Who were the most beautiful movie stars, in your estimation, in your time?''

"Why, I'd say Elizabeth Taylor, Audrey Hepburn, possibly Ava Gardner.''

Edmonds grinned at him again, and said slyly, "How would you like to have a programmed dream in which you took all three of them to bed at once? A dream that was so vivid that it seemed really to be happening, and when you awoke it was in your memory for the rest of your life . . . as if it had really happened.''

"I'll be damned,'' Tracy said.

"Others go for sports,'' Edmonds continued. "Climbing mountains, shooting tigers, winning boxing matches against world champions of the past, winning races in the Olympics. Others like war scenes. Shooting down enemy Fokkers in the First World War, in their Spads, or Messerschmidts in their Spitfires in the Second, becoming Ace of Aces. Others like battles in the trenches, or in the jungles of South Vietnam.''

"Not for me,'' Tracy growled. "I've been there . . . and back.''

Edmonds went on. "Still others like to return in time. They take over Alexander's command of the battle of Issus against Darius the Persian or that of Cortes in the conquest of Tenochtitlan. That, by the way, is an interesting aspect. If you wish, you can change history and have Montezuma win over the Spanish Conquistador. Almost always, of course, you are the central character and the hero. Hardly ever, though it is possible, do you fail to come out winner of all."

Tracy said doubtfully, "You mean it's possible for the dream to go wrong?"

"Oh, no," Edmonds told him. "You get what you want. But occasionally someone wants an experience in which he fails." He laughed. "I knew a chap once who, just to be perverse, wanted, in his dream, to pursue the most beautiful girl in the world and then, in the end, in bed with her, he required that he couldn't get an erection."

Tracy thought of something. "Back there you noticed that an extra building had been devoted to these programmed dreams and you didn't like to see it. Why not?"

"Because programmed dreams are addictive. People get hooked on them. They return again and again. After a while, their real lives hold no interest for them. Aside from waking long enough to eat, exercise, and get a little real sleep, they spend all the time they can going through dream after dream. It's rather frightening, the ramifications of it."

"Have you ever done it?" Tracy said, looking at the other quizzically.

"Oh, yes. Several times. But no more, for me. I want to hang onto reality. However, I recommend it to you . . . just for the experience. For once or twice. Come on in and I'll show you how it works."

Tracy followed him into the building. It looked like an averagely swank hotel, complete to a reception desk, which didn't, however, have a clerk behind it. On the desk sat a screen.

Edmonds approached the screen and said something into it, and it answered. Tracy didn't catch the words.

Edmonds said, "This way, Tracy. We're lucky to have gotten a room immediately, but I told them it was just for two hours."

Tracy followed him down a corridor and to a room. Once again, it looked more like a hotel room than anything else. Edmonds closed the door behind them.

Tracy said, being somewhat nervous about all this, "No bad after effects, eh? No hangover?"

"No aftereffects at all, "the other reassured him, "except for the rest of your life you'll have the memory. What do you want to dream about for the next two hours? By the way, the same amount of time will elapse in your dream."

Tracy thought about it. "Damned if I know."

"Well, take your pick."

Chapter Nine

Tracy said, "Well, one thing that's always intrigued me was the gardens of Hasan Ben Sabbah."

Jo Edmonds said, "Never heard of him. Stretch out on the bed here. You can do this yourself, after the first time. I'll show you how."

Tracy obeyed orders. "Nothing can go wrong, eh?"

"Nothing can go wrong."

Edmonds put electrodes on both of Tracy's eyes and one at the nape of his neck. "The idea is," he explained "to send low-frequency pulses to your cerebral cortex. All right, now tell all you know about this Hasan-whatever-his-name-was and about those gardens of his."

Tracy said, "I read a biography about him while I was in a concentration camp. Hasan Ben Sabbah was a contemporary of Omar Khayyam, the poet. In fact, they went to school together and were friends. Hasan became head of the Persian sect of the Ismailian Moslems and began a reign of terror in the country. He seized the castle of Alamut on a mountain just south of the Caspian Sea, and it was there he built possibly the most fabulous gardens ever known. When the Crusaders came, he was known to them as the Old Man of the Mountain. He became the most powerful force in Persia. This is how his system worked. He would take one of his younger, stronger—and more stupid, it's to be assumed—men and feed him some hashish. The follower would pass out and when he awakened find himself dressed like a Prince from the Arabian Knights. He would be in beautiful gardens the fountains of which gushed wine, supposedly forbidden by Allah on Earth, but available in abundance in paradise. The walks of these fabulous gardens were graveled with precious and semiprecious stones. The buildings were probably similar to those later erected by the Moors in Spain in Grenada, the Alhambra.

''The follower was a simple Arab. He probably came from a small desert town, or had been born in nomad tents. This to him was inconceivable. The most water he had probably ever seen in his life would have been only enough to quench his thirst. He had probably never been clean before in his life. But the baths and fountains here were everywhere. On top of all else, there were eight of the most beautiful women he had ever even dreamed of, and they came in a wide selection of flavors. And they all adored him. They were obviously the houris promised by Mohammed for each man when he entered paradise. They were supposedly not truly human—because the Moslem woman does not enter paradise, but only the man—but each was more beautiful than any woman on Earth. At least, the Hasan follower must have thought so, probably never having seen a truly beautiful woman in his life, certainly not unveiled.

"On him they pressed the most delicious food he had ever eaten. They vied for his favors. They continued to ply him with hashish. They played exotic music for him, sang softly to him, saw he was most comfortable on his cushions. And, above all, they submitted him to every sexual act known at the time . . . and they knew as much then as ever before or after.

"Before he became seated, they gave him still more hashish so that he passed out again. When he awakened, he was back in the presence of Hasan Ben Sabbah, in that worthy's throne room. The follower was again in his original dirt and rags, and probably had a hangover, at least a slight one, from the unaccustomed wine, the rich food, the sex, and the hashish.

"Hasan explained to him gently that he had just been to paradise, just as a sample of what would be his for all eternity if he but followed the commands of Hasan Ben Sabbah, leader of all the faithful Ismailians. Upon death, in the service of Hasan, he would immediately return to paradise and his eight houris. Obviously, the simple countryman swore devotion.

"Hasan would then dispatch him to assassinate this vizier, this sheik, or that emir, who was currently standing in the way of Ismailian ambitions. When it comes to assassination, there is little defense against a man who is willing to die in the attempt. Or, if there was a successful defense against the first one, another assassin came, and a third, and a fourth. And finally the proposed victim either got the message and made his peace with Hasan, or, sooner or later, he fell to the knives of the assassins.

"The origin of the word assassin is debated. It is evidently either derived from 'Hasan' or 'hashish' the drug he befuddled his followers with."

"To use your favorite term, Jesus Christ," Jo Edmonds said. "Just what do you want to dream doing in this garden of Hasan Ben Sabbah?"

Tracy said, "I want to enter it exactly as did his drugged followers. I'll have to be able to speak Arabic or Persian, or whatever it was they spoke in Omar Khayyam's time. Either that, or whoever I meet will have to speak English."

"That's no problem," Edmonds said. "All right. Here you go." He reached over to the small table beside the bed and flicked a switch.

Tracy was seated on a large, elaborately carved low wooden stool which was highly encrusted with jewels and inlayed with mother-of-pearl. The cushion he sat upon was embroidered with gold thread and with pearls. He was dressed in silken, baggy trousers, a richly embroidered vest-like jacket, wore a red silken turban on his head, and was shod in beautifully soft suede slippers, the toes of which turned up.

He had no memory of his past and, for the moment, no interest in anything save his immediate future. Somewhere in the near distance was the sound of swirling music.

He came to his feet and made his way in that direction. He was slightly high but not to the point where any of his senses were dulled. In fact, all of his senses were highly alert. The path which he followed was graveled with highly colorful stones of a score of varieties. He stooped and picked one up. It was a beautiful black opal, polished. Pleased with it, he put it in the dark velvet sash which encircled his waist, then stooped again and picked up a red stone which flashed light quite brilliantly. A garnet, or possibly a ruby, he thought. But it didn't please him as much as the black opal had and he tossed it away. He stooped still once again and picked up an oval-shaped green stone. It came to him that it must be jade. Something flickered in his mind, a memory, but he rejected it and proceeded along the walk rubbing the piece of jade between a thumb and forefinger.

The path passed a fountain. In its center was a golden lion which spouted from its mouth some red fluid. There was a golden cup sitting on the fountain's edge. It was beautifully worked and encrusted with cut jewels of red, blue, and green rubies, sapphires and emeralds.

He took the cup up, dipped it into the fountain, and then sipped at the contents. A red Bordeaux, very similar to Chateau Haut-Brion, he decided, although his memory gave him no inkling of where he had ever tasted the French wine. Though the drink was superlative, he didn't pause to sample it further, but put the cup down and continued his way toward the music.

There was heavy natural fragrance in the air, undoubtedly due to the profusion of flowers. He could recognize only a few of them: roses, violets, lilacs, jasmine, bougainvillaea. The roses were in various colors and all surpassingly large and perfect; there was no sign of wilt on any of them.

There were hedges, ferns, trees of various species, including palm, all perfectly trimmed. The grass on the lawns was as that on the putting greens of a first-class golf course, though, once again, his mind refused to bother with the matter of where he had seen a golf course.

He passed several small buildings in the Persian tradition from the days of Tamerlane. Bougainvillaea, jasmine, and ivy climbed the walls; there were domes of blue, green, and gold tile; the doors and windows were horseshoe shaped, sided with pink-hued marble.

He passed through a massive gate. It was horseshoe-shaped, possibly twenty feet high and wide enough so that four cavalrymen abreast could have ridden through it without crowding.

Before him stretched a court some one hundred fifty feet long by seventy-five feet wide. In the center was a large pond set in the marble pavement. There were myrtles growing along its side, and they were being well cared for. In the pond were tropical fish of every hue. There were galleries on the north and south sides of the court; that on the south was about twenty-five feet high and supported by a marble colonnade. Underneath it to the right was what Tracy assumed was the principal entrance to the buildings proper. Over it were three elegant windows with highly decorated arches and miniature pillars, once again in colored marble. And it was in this direction from which the swirling music was coming.

The room beyond was a perfect square, about twenty-five feet to the side and with a lofty dome and trellised windows at its base. The ceiling was decorated with blue, brown, red, and gold tiles, and the columns supporting it sprang out into an arch in a remarkably beautiful manner.

He pressed on and passed into another patio, one even more elaborate than the first. It seemed to be some one hundred feet in length by sixty-five feet in width and was surrounded by a low gallery supported by a good many pure white marble columns. A pavilion projected into the court at each extremity, with filigree walls and light-domed roofs, elaborately decorated with openwork. The square was paved with colored tiles, and the colonnade with white marble, while the walls were covered five feet up from the ground with blue and yellow tiles, with a broader above and below of enameled blue and gold. In the center of the court was a fountain with a magnificent alabaster basin.

The music was coming from the pavilion to the right, the largest of the four which projected into the court. And before it, six girls twirled in a graceful dance, seemingly unaware of his approach.

On his way toward them, Tracy passed the alabaster fountain and its bouquet wafted over to him. The spray was slightly yellowish in color, and the odor was of the Moselle. He would have guessed possibly a Trocken-beerenauslese, though, once again, his memory told him nothing of where he would have picked up information about such a germanic wine.

Upon his approach, two of the dancing girls darted

toward him, laughing; they captured his arms and laughingly dragged him toward the pavilion, the other four giggling behind, bringing up the rear.

The pavilion was largely furnished with low couches, piled high with pillows and cushions. And it was from here that the music had been coming: Two girls were playing long-necked stringed instruments.

Tracy looked at them, eight of them in all. They were dressed in diaphanous silken trousers and gilted slippers, similar to his own with the upturned toes; all were topless. Their clothing differed only in color; pink, blue, red, orange, purple, green, brown, gold. Their figures above the waist were exceptional, and, in actuality, little was left to the imagination about the rest of them, in spite of the voluminous ankle-length trousers. They were so transparent that even the pubic hair could be seen.

The pubic hair differed. By guess, Tracy Cogswell decided that one of the girls, the most petite, was Chinese; and her hair was dark black. Another was possibly a Finn, very blonde, with very blue eyes. Another was probably Hindu, brown-eyed; a precious stone, possibly a diamond, was set into the side of her nose, and there was a caste mark on her forehead. Still another was a Negress, ebony skined, the plumpest of the eight; she had Caucasian features. He suspected she was Ethiopian, of Hamitic descent. Another was probably Arab and had sloe, sensuous eyes. Another, a green-eyed goddess, platinum blonde hair, he would have thought English; her legs were remarkably long. Still another had flaming red hair, both on her head and in her pubic region; he suspected she was Circassian but couldn't be sure. The last of the eight: Could she possibly be Texan, or Californian, with that seemingly corn-fed figure? For some reason, it seemed unlikely to him, in this atmosphere, and he continued to refuse to think about past memories.

One of those who had him by the arm whispered, "Be seated, Master," and urged him to the principle divan.

Another snatched up a golden goblet and hurried for the fountain from which the Moselle wine gushed. It was a pleasure to watch her graceful run.

Seated, the Hindu girl, her eyes demurely down, proffered a golden tray with several small dishes. She took up a tidbit from one of them and hesitantly put it between his lips. It was a date, stuffed with pine nuts and various spices. He had never tasted any sweetmeat so delicious.

The girl with the goblet, the red-headed Circassian, came scurrying back, holding it in presentation to him in both hands. She sank to her knees before his divan.

Out of his consciousness came a term, though he didn't know in what language he was speaking. "Jesus!" he said.

There were just too many of them. Eight.

Evidently, they anticipated this. One of them said, breathlessly, "Would you like us to dance for you, Master?"

"Yes, of course," he told her.

The two girls who had been playing with the outlandish-looking instruments took them up again and this time they sang, as well. It was a haunting tune, sweetly rendered.

The English-looking platinum blonde and the American-type girl sprang out to the marble floor outside the pavilion and flowed into a graceful, complicated dance. Surely they were well trained ballet girls; they didn't miss a step. They could have been part of a Hollywood production dealing with the Baghdad of the days of Harun-al-Rashid or the Arabian Nights.

The other four girls drooped themselves around him, adoringly. The Hindu girl pressed another tidbit to his lips; it was different from the date, but equally delicious. He took the wine cup from the Circassian and drank deeply from it. It was a fabulous Moselle type, as he has suspected from the bouquet.

The Negress to his left slipped a soft hand into a slit in his trousers all the time staring lovingly into his eyes. The other girls looked miffed that she had gotten to him first. The Arab ran her hand caressingly over his chest, which was bare beneath the embroidered vest.

The Hindu girl murmured into his ear, "Which one of us do you wish to enjoy first, O Master?"

That was a difficult question to answer. All eight of them were superlatively beautiful. Or, at least, they ran the gamut from pretty to unbelievably majestic handsomeness. They were perfect in both face and figure. Surely there had never been a bevy of more attractive girls.

But he had already more than noticed the supreme buttocks of the Hindu girl. They were larger than those of the others, and in spite of the girl's rather darkish complexion, had a rosy quality.

"You," he said to her. He looked about but could see no indication of a bedroom in the vicinity.

But then he realized that the girls didn't expect him to go off seeking privacy with the one of his choice. They expected him to perform here, and with them about.

He said to the Indian, as he moved slightly to one side to make room for her, "Get on your hands and knees."

She drew in her breath and looked ever so slightly apprehensive but did as he commanded.

While the Negress, who had been caressing him most intimately during this, brought his now swollen member from his trousers, the Circassian girl stripped the Hindu's diaphanous trousers away, so that the other was nude. The three who had not been chosen . . . as yet . . . gasped with admiration at his size.

Through this the Chinese and Finnish girls were playing their instruments, and now the song swelled higher and faster. Outside, the dancers swirled faster and faster. Her buttocks were everything he had expected them to be, a wonderful cushion.

Behind him and a little to one side was stationed the Arab. She slyly inserted one small hand inside his trousers. She was an expert and he all but screamed in pleasure. Between the two of them, he came quickly to climax. Much too quickly, but he knew that there would be more. Instinctively, he knew that there was to be no limit to his virility.

He reached over and picked up his glass of wine.

The Negress came scurrying up with a tray of food. He could recognize none of the dishes, but the smell of them all was simply tremendous. He took up a drumstick of some sort of bird: certainly it wasn't chicken, duck, or turkey. Possibly peacock he thought. It was heavy with a sauce which he also failed to recognize, though once again he detected the delicate flavor of pine nuts.

The Hindu girl had weakly begun to get back into her silken trousers.

"Just leave those off," he ordered. "I might want to get into that again."

"Yes, Master," she said.

Chapter Ten

When he awakened, it was to find Jo Edmonds seated in an easy chair about six feet from where Tracy was stretched out on the bed. The other eyed him speculatively, but for the nonce said nothing.

Tracy took a deep breath. "How much of that was real?" he demanded.

"None of it."

Tracy shook his head negatively. "It had to be," he said. "I had that experience as truly as any I've ever had. What do they do, mock up some fabulous sets in some present-day Hollywood and . . .?" But even as he was saying it, he knew it was impossible.

"No," Edmonds said, crossing his legs. "I mentioned the fact that if you wished to general the battle of Issus between Alexander the Great and Darius, you could. Do you think any tri-di or movie set could involve sixty thousand Macedonians and possibly as many as a million Persians? No, none of it happened, or, at least, it happened only in your mind."

"Could I go back?"

The other shrugged. "Yes, again and again, if you wished, and either repeat the same experience or go on from where you left off."

"And the same girls would be there, all eight of them?"

Edmonds laughed softly, "Or a new batch, if you'd prefer, old chap. There's only one proviso. You can't stay in a programmed dream for more than eight hours out of the twenty-four."

"Why not?" Tracy swung his feet around and to the floor preparatory to getting out of the bed.

"For reasons of health," the other told him. "Some addicts are so hooked on programmed dreams that they would remain in them until their bodies starved to death, stretched out on the dreamer's bed. So the Medical Guild has rather insisted that eight hours at a stretch is all that you can take. Of course, if you wish, when you take your next eight hours you can return to the exact split second that your last eight hours ended in. Some do. I knew of one chap who went back to the days of Republican Rome, to Egypt. He went off his trolley with Cleopatra, or at the least with the dream world version of her and spent the rest of his dream life returning over and over again to her. All I can say is, she must have been one bloody special piece of ass."

Tracy said, "When you dreamed, what did you do?"

"None of your business," Edmonds said, flushing slightly.

Tracy snorted slight amusement. "I'll bet one hell of a lot of the dreams are erotic experiences similar to the one I just went through."

"Yes."

Tracy said, "The ramifications of this are stagger-ing, and I've just begun to work them out. Can't the Medical Guild cure the addiction?"

Jo Edmonds was affirmative. He said, "Yes, through an advanced hypnosis technique, involving posthypnotic suggestion. It turns the patient against the programmed dream, though it doesn't erase the mem-ory of the ones he's already had."

"Then why don't they? Why doesn't this Medical Guild of yours take them off of the thing?"

Jo Edmonds said, "Because few programmed dream addicts volunteer for the hypnosis. They don't *want* to be cured. And, you see, they are harming nobody. Nobody at all, except themselves, since the dreams aren't real. You can choose to be Billy the Kid and go back and kill twenty-one men, or however many men he is supposed to have killed. But actually, you would hurt no one. The Medical Guild has no jurisdiction. It's your own silly self that you're hurting and not anybody else."

Tracy was on his feet. He said, "How many people take these programmed dreams?"

"At least hundreds of millions. The Dream Palaces are to be found in every Pleasure Center and there are tens of thousands of Pleasure Centers throughout the world. They are even beginning to spring up where there are no Pleasure Centers, nothing except the Dream Palace. Once onto a Dream Palace, who wants any of the other pleasures offered?"

"All right," Tracy said. "Could we go? That's quite

a wrenching experience, even only two hours of it, and, as you said I would, I remember every bit of it in vivid detail. In short, I'm tired.''

Edmonds took what looked like a silver cigarette case from his pocket and flicked back the lid. ''We should be getting back anyway,'' he said, standing also.

As they returned to the car, Tracy said, ''What's that you looked at, some kind of watch?''

Jo Edmonds said, ''My transceiver. We'll have to get you one tomorrow. In a way it's a watch, since I can get the time on it. But it's a lot of other things, too. It's a two-way TV phone screen in which I can get in touch with anyone in the world, immediately. I can also dial the Universal Data Banks for any information I want. It's also a sort of identification device. Suppose I got lost up in the mountains, or wherever. I'd simply dial, and the computers would get a fix on me, and an automated car would be sent to rescue me.''

They got into the hover-craft and Edmonds activated it.

''That's some device,'' Tracy admitted. ''Does everybody have one?''

''Yes. Everybody who wants one.''

''Why should anybody not want one?''

Edmonds shifted one shoulder. ''How should I know? Perhaps he's a recluse, a hermit or something and doesn't want to be bothered with people calling him all of the time. I really don't know. It's not my field, but everyone I know has one.''

Tracy said, ''Continually, when I ask you questions,

176

you tell me that it's not your field. What in the hell is your field, Jo? That is,'' he added sourly, ''besides being the Tracy Cogswell of this century.''

They were airborne now and presumably heading back for Tangier and the Stein home. Edmonds switched over from manual to auto control.

He said, ''I'm a student of the social sciences; anthropology, ethnology, history, archeology, and specializing in socioeconomics.''

They were the subjects in which Tracy himself was particularly interested though he had had precious little formal education. He had read quite widely in them during his various terms in prisons and concentration camps.

He asked, more respect in his voice than he usually gave Edmonds, ''What do you do with it, Jo?''

The other shrugged his slight shoulders and said with a touch of self-depreciation, ''Not much besides working for the organization. After all, it is an outfit trying to overthrow the present socioeconomic system. I wanted to become a teacher, originally, but there was no place for me. There is need for precious few teachers anymore. The autoteachers, hooked to the Universal Data Banks, are far more efficient than any human instructor could be. The few jobs that there are are largely supervisory ones.''

''What would you say the present social system was?'' Tracy said. ''From what I've seen and heard so far it's certainly not communism, socialism, or even technocracy.''

''It's anarchism,'' Edmonds said bluntly.

177

Tracy thought about that for a minute or two before speaking again. When he did, it was to change the subject.

He said, "These Pleasure Centers, what else do you do in them besides shooting dinosaurs, taking narcotics, having group sex and dreaming away your lives?"

Edmonds answered, "Well, for instance, see that building we're passing over? It's a gourmet restaurant, and kind of a club at the same time."

"Restaurant? I thought your cooking was all automated and that you could have sent to your own home any dish ever devised by man."

"Umm," Edmonds responded. "Largely, but not quite. This is a gourmet restaurant with a difference, old chap. They specialize in exotic dishes of a type most persons wouldn't be interested in and the ingredients of which are sometimes difficult to acquire."

"Such as what?" Tracy was intrigued. He had always been a good trencherman himself . . . when he could afford it, which wasn't too very often.

"Why, I ate there exactly once. Once was enough. Among other dishes they had a certain type of small dog, a very fat little dog originally raised by the Aztecs of Mexico for food. Then they had live shrimp."

"Live shrimp?" Tracy couldn't see where that was particularly exotic. "You mean fresh shrimp, alive before they cooked them?"

"No, I mean shrimp that were alive when they ate them. It's evidently an old Japanese delicacy. You take very small live shrimp and put them in soy sauce and another ingredient or two and they are served under a bowl on top of a dish. The trick is to reach in and get one before he can hop out, bite off his head, and skin the meat out through the shell. It's a bit tricky getting hold of them since they flip-flop all over the place.''

"Jesus. How do raw shrimp taste?''

"I wouldn't know,'' Edmonds admitted. "They also have various types of snakes, including rattlesnakes and cobras which the members can look at in their cages before ordering them to be cooked up. But the pièce de résistance, the night I was there, was live monkey brains.''

"You have to be kidding.''

"No,'' Edmonds said. "It's an old Chinese delicacy. The diners sit at a circular table which has a hole cut in the center. The host comes out leading a monkey, or ape . . . it was chimpanzee on this occasion. He circles the table with it, so that the guests can see it. And it is then clamped under the table in such a manner that the top of its head projects through the hole there. The top of the skull is then sawed off and the diners take their spoons and dip into the brains and eat them.''

"I won't repeat that you have to be kidding,'' Tracy said, nauseated. "You sound too convincing. But I thought you people didn't eat real meat any more, that it was all factory raised, in overgrown test tubes, or whatever.''

"These gourmets like to eat living things,'' Edmonds said grimly. "They like to see the things they

179

are going to eat, still alive. I think they get some sort of a thrill from that. I believe some of them like to do the killing, an atavistic thrill.''

"Okay. What other kind of entertainment do you have in these Pleasure Centers?''

"Oh, various, don't you know. Just about any pleasure that has come down through history. During the daylight hours there are bullfights, cock fights, bull baiting, pit dog fights, bear baiting.''

"Bear baiting?'' Tracy said. "I thought that went out in the Middle Ages.''

"It's been brought back,'' the other told him. "They turn a bear loose in a pit and send in fighting dogs, mastiffs, bulldogs and so forth, to pull it down. Evidently, quite a few people enjoy seeing pain and death inflicted.''

"But bullfighting,'' Tracy protested. "I've seen a bullfight or two, in Spain and Mexico, in my time. And I can understand a matador of my era going through with it in view of the large pay, if he hit the jackpot. But who would be silly enough to be a matador today, when he doesn't have to be?''

Edmonds shrugged again. "People who get a thrill out of it. Or people who get a thrill appearing before a cheering audience. Largely exhibitionists, I should think. The same as with the gladiators.''

"What gladiators?'' Tracy said, looking over at the other in complete surprise.

Edmonds said, "Most Pleasure Centers have arenas patterned after the old Roman ones. In them they duplicate the games of the Romans at the time of the republic and empire. By the way, that's a fallacy that has come down through history. When the Christians took over in Rome, the games didn't end for quite a time. The only difference was that instead of the pagans throwing the Christians to the lions, the Christians threw the pagans. It wasn't until 399 A.D. that the last gladiator schools were closed, although the first Christian emperor, Constantine, had come to power almost a hundred years earlier. In 404 a monk named Telemachus jumped into an arena in Rome and berated the spectators, who were so infuriated that they stoned him to death. The emperor Honorius in turn became so furious over the lynching that he closed the arenas."

Tracy said, "But gladiators in this day and age. That's ridiculous. Who'd be silly enough——"

"Oh, they seldom, if ever, fight to the death. They're probably, as with matadors, sadists, masochists, and exhibitionists. They're consenting adults. If one of them gets hurt, he was asking for it. I'm sure it's not as all-out as it was in the Roman times. Except, of course, the animals they kill with everything from spears to bows and arrows."

"All right. What else?"

"Oh, the less far-out entertainments. Bars, nightclubs, dancing places, that sort of thing. And sports, certainly. Just about all fun and games are represented in a Pleasure Center."

They were coming up on Gibraltar now. The lights on the rock flickered ahead of them.

Tracy said, "What's Gib nowadays? In my time it was a British naval base."

"It's another Pleasure Center. We went on up to Torremolinos because it's a larger one. Gibraltar is too limited in space. There's another one in Rabat, one in Cadiz, one in Seville."

"In short, they're all over the place, eh?"

"Yes," Edmonds nodded. "They're all over the place and more are being built all the time. More and larger ones. Especially the Dream Palaces."

Tracy said, "That brings something to mind. Back there you said that nothing in my programmed dream was reality. It was all in my head. But that can't be right. For instance, I know nothing at all of the architecture of Persia in Omar Khayyam's time, but I saw it there. I also know nothing about the musical instruments and the music of the time, but I saw and heard them. You also said I could go back and be Alexander at Issus, but I know nothing about the battle of Issus. I don't even know Greek, so I couldn't have ordered the troops around."

Edmonds replied, "I gave you a wrong impression. When you're having a programmed dream, you're tied in with the data banks, which, of course, have all the information known to man in them, including the architecture, music and everything else of old Persia. They also have all information known about the Battle of Issus, including the types of weapons used on both sides, and including the types of chariots utilized and even including the breeds of horses current at the time. So far as speaking Greek is concerned, the data bank computer translators can translate any known language

182

into any other immediately. Or, for that matter, they could change history around a bit and have both the Greeks and Persians speaking Interlingua or English.

"So what happens is, you speak into the mike telling all you know about what you want, as you did about Hasan Ben Sabbah and his gardens, and when you drop off into your dream, the computers take over."

Tracy shook his head in wonderment, as he had been doing so often these past few days.

They had passed over the Straits of Hercules and now the pilot took over manual controls again.

Tracy indicated the hover craft. "How do these things work? Sooner or later, I'll have to know."

"Oh, they're quite simple and quite safe, Tracy," Edmonds said. "You could hardly have an accident if you wanted to. In case of danger, the computers take over immediately, even if you're on manual control." He pointed out the method of starting up, the lift lever, the accelerator, what amounted to a brake.

Tracy said, "How about this automatic stuff?"

"That's simplest. "You first dial the coordinates of your destination and the computers, once again, take over."

"Yeah," Tracy said. "But suppose you don't know the coordinates of your destination?"

"Then you simply dial Information and ask for them. I usually like to land and take off manually, but there's no real need of it, I shouldn't think. The hover craft would have landed at exactly the point before the garage where we took off from the Stein house. There's a landing pad there. If there is no automated landing pad where you wish to go, you must switch over to manual and land yourself."

They were approaching the Stein home and now whisked in to a landing. They went on into the living room and found Betty Stein, wrapped up in a night robe with a drink handy to her on a cocktail table, watching the life-size tri-di screen which took up the greater part of one wall. She flicked the set off when they entered.

She looked at Tracy, bit of mockery in her eyes. "Well," she said. "And did you have fun?"

"Yes," he told her.

Chapter Eleven

"And what impressed you most about out decadent modern society?" she said.

"The Dream Palaces."

Jo Edmonds yawned and said, "I'm off to sleep. Has the academician already gone?"

"Yes. He took off early." She looked back to Tracy. "He suggested that you pop into bed as soon as you returned, as well. He's still afraid that you'll overestimate your strength. And, if my guess is correct, you probably now feel something like a wet washcloth."

Edmonds, still yawning, drifted off, but Tracy went over to the bar and dialed himself a nightcap.

He came back with it to sit across from her and said, "I do. But I can't understand why. If it didn't really happen, why should I feel tired?"

Her voice still mocking, she said, "How many orgasms did you have?"

He looked at her sourly. "At least six, over a period of two hours time."

"What a man," she said. "Well, the truth is that though your body wasn't really in action, psychologistically the experience happened to you and you feel as tired as you should."

He sipped his drink, then said, "This fascinates me. Look, why do people bother with such things as narcotics, group sex, small-time sadism, and gladiator fights, not to speak of gourmet restaurants? Group sex? I had more group sex in that two hours than ordinarily I could have gone through in a week. And with the most beautiful broads possible. I was even equipped with a super-sized tool, a bigger one than I have in the ordinary world. Sadism? Why bother with a bit of whipping each other? Why not go back to the original, the works of the Marquis de Sade? From what Jo told me, the dream you have doesn't have to have any resemblance to reality, it can be strictly fiction. Gourmet food? Why not go back to the days of Nero and sit in on some of his banquets, instead of eating live shrimp?"

She nodded at the validity of his question and said, "The Dream Palaces have only been going for about five years. They are taking over tremendously. The Pleasure Centers are having a time building them fast enough, even with modern means of construction. They're always packed. But some people haven't got onto the hang of them as yet, to the point of being able to milk the possibilities completely."

He took another pull at his drink and said, "I can't see why these programmed dreams should be all bad. They'd be a wonderful method of education. Why, an anthropologist could go back to Neolithic times and study the Stone Age. A historian could take in at first hand the siege of Troy."

She said, "All the information that would be available to such scholars is in the data banks. You can't get more in a dream than is in those banks."

"Sure," he said doggedly, "but it's the way in which you acquire it. You see, you participate in it. That's a far cry from just reading about it on an autoteacher screen."

"I've heard the point made before," she admitted, "and it has a certain amount of validity for some people. I knew one fellow who started off dreaming he was Columbus first sighting land. It must have been quite a thrill. But that's how the addicts start; soon they go on to more stupendous things. I knew another fellow who first became an Eskimo, hunting seal and walrus, building igloos and that sort of thing. Within a month, he was being Napoleon at Waterloo and defeating Wellington . . . somewhat of a switch on history. That so intrigued him that he fought all of Napoleon's battles, one by one, and from there went on to battles that had never happened. Among other things, he had our little corporal invading North America and conquering the United States, and Canada to boot. What he's dreaming up now, God only knows. I haven't seen him for six months. He spends eight hours out of the twenty-four in programmed dreams. He is in real life just long enough to eat, get minimum exercise, get some true sleep, and then he's back to his dreams. He used to be a notable scholar."

Tracy said, "What happens to those who didn't even

start off being scholars? The ordinary man or woman in the street?''

She said in disgust, ''I had one male friend . . . he used to be a lover of mine . . . who set off to bed every famous beautiful woman in history. He started with Queen Nefertiti of Egypt, wound his way up to Cleopatra and Messalina and then onward to such notables as Agnes Sorel, Madam Du Barry, Catherine the Great, Madame Pompadour, Nell Gwen, and on and on. Finally, he ran out of names of the most beautiful women he knew of and began studying up on the subject. He went down the list, reading all he could find in the data banks on famous courtesans, prostitues and such. One by one he bedded them all. Then he got into fictional characters. You'll never believe this, he even took on Minnie Ha Ha, the Indian princess girl friend of Hiawatha.''

''He must have had a time for himself,'' Tracy laughed, finishing his drink.

''That's right,'' she said bitterly. ''But he no longer had time or desire for real women. He was no longer my lover, nor anyone else's in the real world.''

''Yeah,'' Tracy said, standing. ''I got the implications when you were telling me the story. There must be quite an impact on the birth rate.''

''Birth rate,'' she said, still bitterly. ''What birth rate?''

He had been about to leave, but now he came to a halt. ''What do you mean?''

''I mean that the birth rate has been falling off to the vanishing point. It's not just that our most potent men

188

spend so much time living it up in harems in Turkey or Araby, but we women aren't exactly immune. There are those among us who would rather spend a night with Hercules or Paul Bunyon than with a truly live, breathing, normal man.''

"Jesus," he said.

"Yes, but that's not the all of it. The Dream Palaces are only one factor. Who in this hedonistic world of ours wants to go through the trouble of childbirth and raising a child? A decreasing number. Frankly, I have no special desire in that direction myself. And I'm comparatively conservative.''

He stared at her.

"And now," she said, and the mocking quality was back in her voice again, "I assume that you are not particularly interested in my accompanying you to your bed tonight. Not in view of the fact that you have experienced more than six orgasms . . . in your mind.''

"No, I suppose not," he said. "Good night, Betty. This sort of thing isn't going to happen to me again.''

"We'll see," she said. "You've already let us know that so far what you've seen of this society you rather like.''

"I'll talk about it with the three of you tomorrow," he said. "Good night, again.''

He made his way to his room, but instead of undressing he stretched out on his bed, fully clothed and stared up at the ceiling.

So, it was for this that he had devoted his life to the movement. It was for this he had fought in half a dozen

189

wars, revolutions, and revolts. It was for this that he had been wounded more times than he could remember. It was for this that he had spent years in prisons and concentration camps.

And all his friends who had stood shoulder to shoulder with him. All those who had died in the struggle. Jim Farthington and Bud Whiteley, in the Spanish Civil War; Ferry Washington, who had been lynched in Mississippi; Buck Dillard, Dave Woolman, Fred Thompson, all dead fighting Hitlerism in the Second World War; Ilya Rostov and Michael Manovich, caught by the Soviets and last heard of in a Siberian labor camp; Luca Memmi and Lippo Signorelli, dead with the partisans, fighting Mussolini in Northern Italy. Yes, and many more, and above all, Dan Whiteley, who evidently had been shot after Tracy had gone into hibernation, or whatever you wanted to call it. Shot by the Maoists in Communist China when he was trying to get the movement going there.

All of them dead, and many more. But they were the dead. Hundreds and thousands of others in the organization Tracy had belonged to had been caught and imprisoned for varying terms, some of them for life.

Yes, all of the martyrs. The men and women who had given all there was to give, fighting for a cause, a better world, a Utopia.

Well, here it is, Tracy Cogswell. Here is the Utopia you all fought for.

His mind went back again over the list of those who had been close to him and had gone down in the fight, and as before, he ended the list with his best friend.

190

The last time he and Dan Whiteley had worked together to any extent had been in Budapest in 1956 when the revolution was on there. Otherwise, he hadn't even seen Dan except for those times in the Tangier medina.

Tracy was even more tired than he had realized. He fell off into sleep, still clothed, still thinking about Dan Whiteley.

Chapter Twelve

And the dream that came to him was almost as vivid as the one he had gone through in the gardens of Hasan Ben Sabbah . . . but hardly as enjoyable.

Tracy Cogswell and Dan Whiteley had both been in Vienna when the anticommunist Hungarian revolution of 1956 began.

Tracy was already permanently attached to the organization in Tangier, and Whiteley had been working with the Solidarity branch of the movement in England; but both had been sent to Austria in an attempt to strengthen the organization there. The Austrians, they found, were on the easy going side when it came to drastic changes in the politico-economic system. Their idea of carrying on a conspiracy was to sit around in one of the little taverns on the outskirts of town, drinking *heurigen wein* whilst eating *wurst*, listening to a zither player somewhere in the background, and talking endlessly about the finer technicalities, such as where Marx and Engels had gone wrong.

Before meeting in Vienna, the two hadn't seen each

other for some time. Dan Whiteley had less than enjoyed a rather remarkable stint in the Second World
War. He had been in England when it started and
immediately signed up, anti-Hitlerite that he was. His
years in Spain didn't do him any good with the British
military authorities and they didn't even make him a
noncom. He had been captured at Dunkirk and, instead
of being sent to a military concentration camp, he had
been sent to East Prussia and assigned to work on a farm
along with one other allied prisoner. The three young
sons who had formerly helped with the farm chores had
been called up by the German army, leaving only their
elderly parents. The two old folk weren't particularly
hard to get along with, but Whiteley had no intention of
sitting the war out in such wise. He and his companion
escaped and, rather than trying to get all the way
through Germany to France or England, headed north
in the direction of Poland. They thought they might be
able to make it across the Baltic to Sweden. Happily,
his companion was of Slavic background and could
speak the language, so when they were captured by the
Polish partisans they made out all right, and Dan spent
two years with them, before his companion was killed
and he was recaptured. The Gestapo decided Dan was
an American who had been parachute dropped to stir up
the Poles, and they worked him over a bit for a confes-
sion and to get him to reveal any other American agents
in the country. He was saved from being shot by the
advancing Red Army, which took the prison in which
he was held.

Yes, it had been quite a war. Dan's biggest regret

was that it was the Russians who had liberated him. By this time, he hated their guts.

Tracy was sitting in their favorite meeting place, the Gosserkeller, a beer hall located at Elisabethstrasse 3, near the Opera, having a stein of the superlative Schwechater *dunkles* beer. He was at a small table off to the side. One of the advantages of the oversized beer hall was that it was so noisy and packed that you could carry on any kind of a conversation whatsoever and nobody would hear you.

Whiteley came in, excitement in his less than handsome face. He took the chair across from his companion.

He said, excitedly, ''Been following the news?''

Tracy snorted and said, ''You mean from Poland? Now that they've brought that old Party hack Gomulka into power, things will simmer down. There won't be any basic changes in spite of all this gobbledygook about his standing up to Krushchev.''

Dan reached across the table and picked up Tracy's stein and took a heavy gulp of the dark beer. He said, ''I mean from Budapest.''

''What's happened now?'' Tracy said cynically. ''I understand that they're bringing Imre Nagy back into power, kicking Mayyas Rakosi out. But so what? Nagy's just another Communist party hack.''

Dan Whiteley was jubilant. He said, ''You should have heard the radio this morning. Hellsapoppin in Budapest. All over the country, for that matter. Tracy, this is it. All Hungary is up. The students, the teachers, the intellectuals, and the workers are forming worker's

194

councils to take over production. Even the army has come over. Pal Maleter is heading the army. They've all come in. Hell, even the church. Cardinal Mindszenty is backing the revolt, getting into the act . . . they have to. Tracy, this is it. The people are taking over! I'll spread. If Hungary goes, Czechoslovakia will be next, then Poland, East Germany. It'll go both East and West. Spain, Portugal, Rumania, Yugoslovia to begin with. Eventually, the world. The people are taking over!''

Tracy said, "For Christ's sake. Let's go back to the hotel. I want to hear the latest developments.''

They were staying in a small pension on Schellin Gasse, two blocks over from the Schubert Ring in an older part of the town. For economy reasons, they shared a room and took all of their meals at the pension rate. They walked, to save the cab fare, but they walked fast. It was only five or six blocks.

Even as they strode, Tracy said, "What's the AVO in Hungary doing about all this?''

"The Security Police? There's fighting going on in the streets, but evidently they're scared spitless. Hundreds of thousands of students, workers and whoever, and his cousin, are out in the streets. When they catch an AVO man they shoot him and usually string him up to the nearest lamppost.''

"It couldn't happen to nicer people,'' Tracy growled.

"They're evidently storming the Budapest radio station in Sandor street. The broadcasts coming from it are really typical commie. They claim the revolt is being headed by foreign fascists and secret agents from the United States.''

''Typical is right,'' Tracy snorted.

Dan said excitedly, ''A big strong point is the industrial area of Czepel Island in the Danube between Buda and Pest. It seems the people from there stormed an arsenal and armed themselves.''

''Jesus,'' Tracy said.

They reached the hotel and took the stairs two at a time.

They flicked on the radio. Dan sat on one of the beds, Tracy straddled a chair backwards, and they stared at the speaker.

Since Spain, and the formation of the organization, Tracy had become the more dominant of the two, even though he was younger. His dedication was strong and for years he had been working full-time for the movement. Dan was utilized often, when his expenses could be met by the meagre organization treasury, but he didn't have quite the reputation that Tracy did.

Finally, Tracy reached over and flicked the set off. He looked at his friend and colleague. He said, ''We're going to have to get on over there, Dan.''

Dan Whiteley licked his lips. ''Yeah. I guess so. Should we check with the Executive Committee?''

''No time. Besides, we're on the scene, and they aren't. We'll have to play it by ear.''

''What's our cover?'' Dan said.

''The same as it is now. We're American journalists. Nobody ever shoots a journalist. Not on purpose. It causes too much of an international stink.''

Dan said sarcastically, "A hell of a lot of good a stink does you after you've been shot. Who's our contact in Budapest?"

Tracy said, "Damned if I know. Franz Zieglar would know. We'll get in touch with him. I don't think we have many members in Hungary. It's like the other commie countries. Hard to organize there."

Dan said, "You ever been in Budapest?"

"No."

"I was there once. Few days. Great town. Good food, good booze. Nice people . . . in a Hungarian sort of way. They say that Hungarians are the only people who can go into a telephone booth and leave by a rear entrance."

Tracy laughed and said, "The way I heard it was that they were the only people in the world that could go into a revolving door behind you and come out in front."

Dan left to go to the public phone out in the hall and call Franz Sieglar, one of the local Austrian organization men.

While he was gone, Tracy growled to himself. "I'll bet it's a great town, these days. Gypsy music and everything . . . played from the top of Joseph Stalin tanks."

Franz Zieglar was efficient, as Austrians went. About forty years of age, plump, and innocent looking, he was one of the organization's liaisons between the western groups and Czechoslovakia, Hungary, Yugoslavia, Rumania, and Bulgaria. He had a beautiful cover. He owned a small antique shop on the Kohlmarkt, just behind the Hofburg former Imperial Palace.

He periodically made shopping trips to Budapest, Prague, and Belgrade, quite legitimately. His specialty was buying antiques, old paintings, and first editions from former aristocrats now on their uppers and unable to get employment. They would often have something valuable, left over from the old days, and would sell it for very little, by western standards. Zieglar broke no laws in so buying. The local Communist governments were glad to have him bring hard western currency into the country . . . sooner or later it would wind up in their coffers.

He gave Tracy and Dan a complete rundown on the state of the movement in Hungary, and particularly in Budapest. Tracy had been correct, there weren't many members, and most of them were concentrated in the capital and most were intellectuals; that is, writers, artists, teachers, students. There were a few engineers and technicians out in the industrial towns such as Miskolc, Gyor, and Pecs. In fact, one member was a factory manager in Szolnok.

Their immediate contact was to be a poet named Gyula Rajk, who belonged to the Petofi Circle.

"A poet!" Dan said in disgust.

Franz Zielgar looked at him. "The poet's art is more highly regarded in Eastern Europe than it is currently in England and America."

Tracy said, "What's the Petofi Circle?"

Zieglar turned his eyes to the American as though he couldn't believe the question had been asked.

"The Petofi Circle! Why, it's the group that started this whole thing. It was begun in April of this year, organized by students and members of the writer's union. They brought out the *Irodalmi Ujsag*, the Literary Gazette, and from the first they criticized the bureaucratic interference with the writer's freedom. Their meetings were soon attracting thousands of people."

"All right. Okay," Tracy said. "We'll check ourselves out on that more when we get there. Now, what do you think of our going in as journalists?"

"Every newspaperman based in Vienna is either already in Budapest or is heading there. And more are being flown in from Paris, London, and everywhere else, by the minute. They fly here to Vienna and then take cars to Budapest. It's about a hundred and eighty miles."

"And they don't stop them at the border?"

"The border is chaos. Nobody knows who is in charge, and thousands of refugees are crossing every day. The damned Russians stand around looking blank; representatives of the government have made themselves scarce, as the American expression goes; and the new worker's councils, student councils, and so forth are too badly organized as yet to do anything even if they wished to. Which reminds me, foreign correspondents are extremely welcome in Budapest right now. The new uprising there wishes the world to know what is going on." He took a deep breath and added, "They are apprehensive of the Russians."

"They'd better be," Tracy muttered.

The three of them were seated about a small table in the hotel room. Tracy took up the bottle of Enzian

199

brandy which Dan had bought when they first arrived in Vienna. It had turned out to be repugnant stuff in spite of it being the national spirit, so most of it was still left, though in their time both Tracy and Dan had drunk some pretty repugnant stuff. Now he poured them each a stiff drink into water glasses.

He said to Zieglar, "Is there any way you could get us a couple of guns? We didn't bring any when we came to Austria. Afraid they might shake us down at the border and newspapermen aren't expected to be heeled. Besides, we didn't figure there'd be any need for them on this mission."

The Austrian unwrapped a paper package he had brought with him and pushed two holstered pistols toward them. They were heavy-calibered military weapons in heavy black leather sheaths, both of which carried a compartment for an extra clip.

"Walter P thirty-eights," Zieglar said. "Are you acquainted with the operation of the P thirty-eight?"

"Yes," Dan said wryly. "We're acquainted with every goddamned gun that's ever been fired."

Tracy looked at him. It wasn't the sort of thing that Dan said and his tone wasn't as diplomatic as he should have used to an organization member, particularly one who was cooperating as well as this one was. But then he shook his head within himself. It didn't mean anything. Of course they had handled the P.38, and this, and that, and the other weapon. It was like asking if you knew how to utilize a Litz hand grenade. You knew how to put on a Merry Widow condum, didn't you? You weren't entirely ignorant.

Tracy said, flicking the magazine from the butt of the gun, "Where did you get these?"

Zieglar had been slightly miffed by Dan's tone. He said indignantly, "I am a Jew. Before the Nazis there were tens of thousands of Jews in Vienna. When they left there were exactly two hundred and forty-three of us left, all in hiding. The last days, before the allied troops came in, we arose and joined with the partisans in the street fighting. I acquired the guns at that time."

Dan was flicking the 9mm cartridges from the clip of his gun with his right thumb. He said, "Over ten years ago. Have they remained loaded all that time? The springs in the magazines——"

"No. Of course not," Zieglar said. "The magazines have been empty, so the springs would not weaken, and the guns have been kept well oiled. I cleaned them up just before coming over here."

"Good," Tracy said. "You are to be complimented, Franz. How about transportation?"

Zieglar thought for a minute, sipping at his brandy absently. He said finally, "Georg Haslauer has his old Mercedes. It is over twenty years old but he is very proud of it and has kept it in good shape. I would think he would . . . loan it to the movement."

Tracy said, "If anything should happen to it, the organization would reimburse him. Now this fellow Gyula Rajk, the poet. Does he speak anything besides Hungarian?"

"Both German and French. That's why he's the international contact man. Nobody speaks Hungarian

201

except the Hungarians. It's an impossible language. The only tongue it is remotely similar to is Finnish.''

"All right," Tracy said. He had reloaded the clip of the gun and now thrust it back into the butt of the P.38. The gun was unique, as automatics go, being double action; and it wasn't necessary to cock it before firing. He jacked a bullet into the breach and lowered the hammer. Dan had already done the same. They buckled the pistols to their right hips, under their coats.

Tracy was saying, "How do we contact him?"

"Every day he checks with the tourist receptionist at the Danu Hotel, which is located at Apaczai Cseri Janos ut four, right on the Danube River on the Pest side, and about eight blocks below the Parliment building. The receptionist is also a member of the organization and is used as a clearinghouse for the movement.''

"Would it be practical for us to stay there?" Dan asked.

The other nodded. "Yes. The Danu is an Ibusz hotel. That's the national foreign tourist bureau. The girl speaks English.''

"All right," Tracy said again. He sighed. "Could you see about getting the Mercedes from George, whatever his last name is?''

The Viennese came to his feet. "Georg Haslauer," he said. "I'll go immediately.''

The Mercedes was forthcoming. Tracy and Dan stocked up well with canned food. They had no way of knowing how available it might be in Budapest, in the midst of a revolution. They had been in similar situations before and knew by experience that rations could get short in a large city when all chips were down.

202

They drove east, crossing the Austro-Hungarian border at Hegyeshalom, then bowling down the partly finished concrete motorway to the capital city.

Zieglar's description of the border crossing had been surprisingly accurate. There was a gate there and customs and immigrations buildings, but both were deserted so far as officials were concerned. To both left and right of the road and buildings were stretches of barbed wire as far as the eye could see. To each side of the road were Russian T-34 medium tanks; the leather-helmeted crews stood or sat outside them and didn't seem particularly interested in the long files of refugees crossing the border, largely on foot, their belongings in hand. They were men, women, and children of all ages, from babes in arms to doddering octogenarians. Occasionally, there was a car, truck, or horse-pulled wagon, but they were mostly on foot. How far had they come? Budapest was at least another hundred miles, but, of course, some of them must have started from nearer points.

On the Austrian side of the border, Red Cross and other relief organizations were busy. Buses and trucks periodically came up and loaded the refugees in. There was a mobile canteen which distributed coffee, buns and sandwiches. The Austrians were rallying around, and Tracy was proud of them. Tracy Cogswell and Dan Whiteley drove through the border gate without interruption. There were several Hungarian soldiers there, the Communist red stars ripped from their caps, but they did nothing more than look curiously at the foreigners.

The faces of the two organization men were expressionless as they drove along the endless file of refugees. They had seen refugees before. It was far from a pleasant experience. You couldn't stop, even to help a woman in childbirth. If you stopped, you'd have an occasion to do so every few minutes. Some of the pedestrians were wounded.

They had filled the car's tank to the brim, at the last petrol station on the Austrian side, and had brought two five-gallon jerry cans of gasoline along too. Which was just as well. They saw no signs of any place they could have refueled all the way to Budapest.

They said little, all the way to the beleagured city.

Once Dan said, "What do we do when we get there?"

"Play it by ear," Tracy told him. He inwardly shrugged, rather surprised at the question from one such as Dan Whiteley.

They had no road map. Not that it made a good deal of difference. In Hungary, evidently all roads led to Budapest, and they couldn't have gotten lost if they'd tried. Occasionally, there was a road sign, in Hungarian, German, and French. They passed through exactly one community large enough to be called a town. After the comparative affluence of Germanic Austria, the whole area was as drab as either of them had ever seen. It was worse then war-torn Spain, as bad as the war-torn Poland Dan Whiteley had witnessed.

"Jesus Christ," Tracy growled. "This country could use a revolution."

Dan said, "I understand that after the Nazis were run

204

out, the Russians stripped the Hungarians of just about everything worth taking, from factory machinery to railroad rolling stock.''

"Where do we enter Budapest?" Tracy asked him. "We must be getting near. I hope we get there before dark. It's probably blacked out, and I'd hate to have some trigger-happy revolutionists taking pot shots at us."

Dan said, "The time I was here, I came by train. But we're to the north of the Danube so we'll be entering on the Buda side of the river. Once we get to the river's edge, I'll know where we are."

It went as he said. Buda wasn't very wide, at least to the southwest where they entered. They soon came to the Danube and travelled parallel to it. There were several bridges.

"Where do we cross?" Tracy asked. The streets were packed with people; many of them, especially the younger, had rifles slung over their shoulders. Some even carried submachine guns. On almost every street corner there was a soapbox speaker. It was a revolution all right.

"A little further down," Dan said. "The Lanchid bridge. Franz said the hotel was on the Pest side, right on the river. Seems to me I've seen it. One of the only hotels on the river not blown down when the fighting with the Nazis took place."

The bridge was guarded by a dozen or so armed civilians who were curious but didn't attempt to stop them.

Tracy came to a halt and said, in each language in turn, English, French, and German, "Does anyone here speak .. . ."

One of the men, who carried a 9mm Steyr Solothurn submachine gun and looked to be about eighteen years of age, said in English, "What do you want to know?"

Tracy said, "Where is the Danu Hotel, Comrade?"

The boy said, "Do not call me Comrade. We now call each other Friend. Who are you?"

"We are American journalists," Tracy said easily. "We have come to learn the true facts of the revolution for the American people, Friend."

"It is a privilege to assist you, Friend," the boy said. "The Duna Hotel is to the right, perhaps three hundred meters. There are many other western journalists there, from many countries." And then he added the international ending of all directions. "You can't miss it."

Tracy and Dan turned right and drove the indicated distance, along the edge of the river. The hotel soon loomed before them. It was a swank hotel, with a beautiful terrace restaurant out on the side overlooking the river. The medieval part of Buda was directly across the stream, and it was unbelievably attractive in the fading light. To their surprise, the restaurant was getting a good play. The tables were packed and there was even a gypsy trio playing away as though half of the patrons didn't have firearms leaning against the tables.

"Jesus," Tracy said.

They parked the car before the entrance and got out. There was no doorman, no bellhops.

Dan said, "Think we ought to leave our bags in the car, with nobody around?"

Tracy said, even as he headed for the door, "You know something? I've never heard of anything being stolen during a revolution. Looting stores and so forth, yes. But nothing personal."

Dan grunted and said, "You better wait until you get the message on what happens when Fidel's boys take Havana."

Tracy looked at him from the side of his eyes. "I didn't know you were in Cuba." They entered the hotel. The lobby was a bit decrepit, but comfortable looking.

"I was up in the hills with them for a while," Dan said. "The organization sent me in to size them up. They aren't our people. Fidel thinks of himself as an idealist and liberal, but his brother Raul and Ché are commies and sooner or later their faction will take over, especially after the United States lands on them like a ton of bricks, and the only place they have to turn is Russia."

The Ibusz tourist reception desk was immediately to the right of the entry. Tracy and Dan approached it.

Behind it was the most beautiful girl Tracy had ever seen. She looked like Hedy Lamarr, back when Hedy was in her prime. Her hair was so black as to seem dyed, but it obviously wasn't; it had too much healthy glisten.

She smiled, took one good look at them, and said in English, "What can I do for you? I am afraid that there

207

are no more accommodations. Reservations are a thing of the past . . . even if you had them. Everything is rather confused. You might try the Gellert Hotel, on the Buda side, but I suspect that they are overflowing as well.''

Tracy said, not sure that this was the right receptionist, ''Franz Zieglar sent us from Vienna. We are to contact Gyula Rajk.''

Her eyes widened and then darted left and right, checking the lobby to see if anyone was within earshot.

She said, hesitantly, ''Then you are from the organization?''

''Yes,'' Dan said laconically. ''Did anyone ever tell you that you looked like Hedy Lamarr?''

''I don't know who Hedy Lamarr is,'' she said, rapidly scanning a ledger before her. She picked up her phone and said something into it rapidly in Hungarian, put it down, and turned back to them. ''I have instructed the desk to put you into a suite that had been reserved for . . . for a committee of friends from Pec who are coming to confer with the local committees of the worker's councils.''

Tracy said, ''I am afraid the organization is in no financial position to——''

''There will be no charge, Friend,'' the girl said simply. ''I am afraid there are no . . . bellhops.''

''We'll get our bags,'' Dan said, already heading for the door.

Tracy paused for a moment and said, ''When will it be possible for us to meet Gyula Rajk?''

''He has been checking in about every two hours,''

208

she told him. "It has been hoped that the organization would send some trained representatives."

"Good."

Tracy and Dan went back to the car to get their two bags and their supply of food. For the time, they decided to leave the Mercedes where it was. There were no other cars around. They'd have to ask the girl where to park it inside. Street demonstrators sometimes had a tendency to burn automobiles just for the hell of it, though the Austrian license plates might give some protection.

Back inside, the girl herself led them up to their appropriated suite. The elevator was not operating.

After she was gone, having promised to send Gyula Rajk up as soon as he made an appearance, Dan looked after her. "I wish the hell all organization members looked like that," he said.

"Yeah," Tracy said, looking about the over-sized suite. "I suppose it's just as well we have a place this size. We might have occasion to hold some meetings."

He went over to the French windows which led out onto a small balcony overlooking the river.

He let himself out and looked down. Dan Whiteley joined him.

Dan said consideringly, "If we have to make a quick get, we could drop from here down to that next terrace, then from there to that awning above the restaurant."

"Ummm," Tracy said. "We'd probably rip right on through the awning, but at least it would slow the drop."

They went on back into the suite and spent the next quarter of an hour cleaning up.

There came a knock at the door. Dan stood to one side against the wall. He unbuttoned the flap on the military holster so that his P.38 Walther was available for a quick draw.

Tracy opened up.

In the hall was a young man of possibly twenty-five, sensitive face, very blue eyes, slight build, his suit on the shabby side. He wore a beret and held a leash in his right hand. On the end of the leash was a moderately large bitch dog.

The newcomer said, "Gyula Rajk."

Tracy opened up, let him in, and closed the door behind them. He said, in German, "I'm Tracy Cogswell, and this is Daniel Whiteley. What in the world are you doing with a dog along?"

The other grinned as they shook hands. He said, "Protective covering. Even with chaos in the streets, who would think to stop a man walking his dog? Give the friends a wag, Plotz."

Plotz gave them a double wag. She was a beautiful dog, reddish in color, her nose red, her eyes golden. Her tail had been bobbed so that it was only about three inches long.

Tracy and Dan looked down at her. "I've never seen the breed," Tracy said.

The newcomer said, "Plotz is a Vizsla. I guess you could call them the Hungarian national dog. They came with the Magyars all the way from Siberia." He put a bottle down on the table in the center of the suite's living room. "Barack," he said.

While Dan went over to a buffet to get glasses, Tracy said, "What's barack?"

The young fellow released the dog from the leash and took a chair at the table. "Hungarian national spirits," he said. "Distilled from apricots."

Tracy Cogswell didn't particularly like liqueurs. "Sweet, eh?" he said. But he didn't refuse it. You must not refuse to drink with a man under these circumstances. It would make for a bad start.

"I've had it before," Dan said. "It's not sweet. It's distilled down until you can just barely recognize the apricot flavor. Strong as vodka."

The three of them knocked back the spirits. After that ceremony was performed, the boy said, "You've heard the latest news?"

Tracy looked at him. "Probably not. We just got in."

"Imre Nagy, supposedly the head of our new government, has invited in the Russian tanks to put down the demonstrations."

Tracy and Dan stared.

"The sonofabitch," Dan blurted.

Tracy slumped back into his chair, his face wan. He sighed deeply and said, "This changes things. I thought possibly we could be of some assistance in forming the new government. To give speeches and so forth, drawing on our years of experience. Possibly write some newspaper articles, that sort of thing."

Dan said bitterly, "We'll be drawing on our years of experience all right, but not in the way of doing speeches and articles."

The tanks didn't come until morning. The Soviets

knew better than to enter narrow streets in the darkness of night. When they came, they came belching cannon fire, plowing through the barricades that the defenders had attempted to throw up during the night. It takes quite a barricade to stop a Joseph Stalin heavy tank, or even a T-34 medium.

When the sound of the firing could first be heard, Tracy and Dan were in a second-floor room of the Polytechnic school giving a talk to thirty or forty young men, all of whom were rifle armed.

Dan was seated to one side, as Tracy spoke.

"Okay," Tracy said. "You're students." He took in a deep draft of air. "I was a student once . . . a long time ago. Now this is what we do. A tank is vulnerable in a city, as the Russians well know, since they took advantage of it in such towns as Stalingrad. Not that I'm bitching about Stalingrad. The Nazis had to be stopped. However, now it's the Russians that have to be stopped. So we'll get around to what you do with tanks in a city."

All of a sudden it came over him, wearily. Yes, he had found out the hard way how you dealt with a tank in a city. So had Dan, here next to him. Yes, Dan knew about how to take a tank in a city.

Tracy went on. "The thing is, that contrary to popular belief the captain of a tank can't fight it efficiently with the hatch down. For any efficiency at all, his head has to be up out of the hatch. That's one thing out on an open plain, but in a city he lays himself open to snipers, so he has to seal up. Besides that, tanks aren't meant for close-up work. That means they can't get their guns leveled on a man who darts right up next to them. And they also run the risk of people in the buildings throwing goodies down on them."

He turned to Dan. "Show them how to make a Molotov cocktail, Dan."

Dan Whiteley had been seated behind a table laden with various pieces of equipment. He came to his feet and took up an empty liter bottle with a screw top. He unscrewed the top, put a small funnel in, then took up the jerry can of gasoline he and Tracy had brought.

As he filled the bottle, he said, in German, "You've probably all heard about the Molotov cocktail. It's one of the simplest weapons you can use against tanks. Larger bottles, such as this, are best but if they aren't available, you can use smaller ones. Try to have a screw top, they're safer, but if they aren't available, a cork will do. Don't try to cork the bottle with a rag. You run the chance of blowing yourself up."

He finished filling the bottle and screwed the top on tightly. He then took up a rag, stripped it to about two inches in diameter and tied it tightly around the bottle. He poured more gasoline on the rag.

"There you are," he said. "Just before you throw it, you light the rag. Your best bet is to throw it from an upper story window, and if possible, and it usually isn't, right into the tank's hatch. If you're out in the streets, run as close as you can get before you heave it. Sometimes one of these will set a tank afire, after all they're gasoline burners."

He thought for a moment before saying, "The piece of rag might be more efficient if you soak it with methylated spirits, if you can get them. And instead of trying it, you can attach it to the bottle with a rubber band, given rubber bands.''

One of the students, who had been stationed at a window said, ''Three tanks and two armored cars are coming up on Szena Square.

Everyone hurried to the windows. All entrances to the square were barricaded, largely with hundreds of barrels, but Tracy and Dan had a few illusions about their efficiency.

The first of the tanks found a weak point and plowed right on through to the center of the square. Large groups of men were firing at it with rifles and a few submachine guns. As Tracy had mentioned, the tank's hatch was closed. Two more tanks, cannons booming, followed after through the same hole, and then two armored cars.

Tracy said to the students, ''Start making up Molotov cocktails. Just as sure as hell they'll break right on through the square and head down this street.''

They began hurriedly to make up the bottles of gasoline.

While they were doing this, Tracy said, ''You remain up here and watch. Dan and I'll give you another lesson in taking a tank in a city.''

He took up a steel crowbar from the table. Dan sighed and took up one of the blankets that were piled on a chair.

Tracy looked at Gyula Rajk, the poet. ''All right,'' he said. ''You can be third man of the team. Take that bucket there and fill it half full of gasoline.''

214

While the other was following orders, Tracy looked around at the remaining students, most of them holding their gasoline bottles. He said, "If we fail, you try raining the cocktails down on them."

One of them, still at the window, called, "One of the larger tanks has broken through the square and is coming down the street."

Tracy said, "Okay. Let's go Dan, Gyula." He led the way to the door, out into the hall beyond, and then down the stairs, explaining the procedure to the poet as they went.

Below, they crouched in one of the doorways of the building, waiting, watching the approaching tank.

"A Joseph Stalin," Dan muttered. "One of the big boys."

"Thank god there's only one of them," Tracy said. "A second one would make mincemeat of us, while we were busy with the first."

Dan looked over at Tracy and grinned wanly and said, "Why did we come all this way to do this?"

"Yeah," Tracy said. "Why?" He grunted. "I didn't ask for it any more than you did."

Dan said, still watching the approaching tank. "A profound thought has just come to me. You know, Tracy, there are two things in this life that a man can only do for himself. Nobody else can do them for him. They are of equal importance."

The poet looked at him, frowning. "What are they?"

"Taking a shit and dying."

The tank, unaware of them, was rumbling closer.

Every so often it would fire its looming gun; at what, the three men didn't know. The streets seemed deserted. The tank crew was probably just proving it was dangerous.

Fortunately, the tank was coming along their side of the street. It was going slowly, cautiously. When it came abreast of them, Tracy darted out and thrust his steel crowbar into the tracks close to the sprocket, thus stopping the vehicle. Dan, immediately behind him, hurled his blanket into the stationary tracks, the poet threw his half full bucket of gasoline onto the blankét, both Dan and Tracy threw fuze matches then turned and darted back for the building again. The tank's gun was already beginning to twirl in their direction.

But then a cheer rang out from the building. The young men were leaning out of the windows, some shaking their rifles. The tank had mushroomed into flame and black smoke.

Tracy yelled up at the boys, "Pot any of them that try to get out."

He and his small team were back inside the building again.

Gyula Rajk looked at Tracy strangely. "But they'd be helpless, possibly even their clothing on fire."

"That's the best time to shoot them," Dan Whiteley growled. "When they're helpless. Let them go, and for all you know they'll wind up in a new tank, shooting at you again. In this kind of fighting, you can't take prisoners, either. We have no facilities for holding them."

The fighting started October 24, a Wednesday, and

by Saturday the Hungarians had knocked out thirty tanks and armored cars. In the long run, it availed them nothing. The Russians hurried in new elements from the north. In some of the towns in the near vicinity of Budapest, the fighting continued until November 14. But a country the size of Indiana does not take on a foe the size of the Soviet Union.

Tracy and Dan called it quits after the first week in November and escaped to the south, crossing over into Yugoslavia, and making their way to Belgrade, still in the guise of journalists. From there they cabled the executive committee and Tracy was returned to Tangier, Dan sent on a mission to South America.

Chapter Thirteen

Tracy awoke just before dawn with a bad taste in his mouth and feeling sticky and dirty from having slept in his clothes. He peeled out of them, considered dialing pyjamas from the distribution center and then decided the hell with it. Nude, he climbed back into the bed. However, he didn't get any more sleep.

He thought back to Budapest. Should he and Dan have stayed on and gone down with the rest of the Freedom Fighters? Gone down before the Russian tanks, as Gyula Rajk, the Hungarian poet organization member had gone down?

No, there would have been no point in that. Dan Whiteley and he had kept in the fighting, training the students and others in guerrilla tactics, participating in the action in the streets, until all possibilities of success were gone. Only then had they fled, to take up the fight elsewhere.

He lay, stretched out there, for two hours, and until daylight; then he came to his feet, and went to the order box, and dialed for fresh clothing from the distribution center, as Betty had shown him. He had no preference and dialed exactly the same clothing he had worn the day before. While waiting for them, he threw the clothes he had the day before into the disposal chute in the bathroom.

He showered, marvelling all over again at the efficiency of the stall. The temperature control, the soap button, the massage units, the pediatric units . . . Christ, they felt good . . . and finally the automatic dryer. He hadn't the vaguest idea of how that operated. It wasn't just warm, dry air. Somehow or other the water on your body just disappeared when you activated the dryer button.

He used the depilatory to remove his facial hair. It was one of the few new advances that really satisfied him. He had always hated shaving, either with soap and razor, or with an electric razor. Now if only you could read while you were going through the routine, it wouldn't be so bad. You simply smeared this stuff, over your face and then immediately wiped it away, complete with whiskers. There was no after-effect, none of the burning he used to feel after a shave. In fact, into the depilatory was even built some sort of astringent which left the face feeling healthy and fresh.

His toilet complete, he went into the other rooms, looking for his hosts. The day was a bit gloomy, by Tangier standards, and they weren't on the terrace but in the breakfast nook, all three of them.

They went through the morning amenities and Tracy seated himself across from Edmonds.

The other three already had food before them. Tracy

had been shown the system of ordering and now dialed for coffee, toast, butter, and marmalade. Over the years, he had become accustomed to the continental breakfast, as opposed to the American ham and eggs, or bacon and eggs, or flapjacks.

While waiting, he looked at Jo Edmonds and said, "Your reason for taking me on our night on the town last night was obvious."

Edmonds nodded. "It was as good a method as any to show you the way the world is going, I should think."

The center of the table sank, and returned, with Tracy's food. He pulled the dishes before him, took up the butter knife and began to butter his toast.

He said, "Okay. I got the message. But the thing is, this society still has a lot going for it. You've eliminated poverty, pollution, the shortage of natural resources, overpopulation, crime . . . just about everything that plagued us in my time, including war."

Walter Stein said thoughtfully, "I would not for a moment condone war, but, for that matter, it is now quite impossible, since we have global unity, and no such things as armies, air forces, or navies exist. But in the past, war was one of the elements that sometimes promoted rapid advances of the race. Take World War One. In 1908 the Frenchman Gabriel Voisin made what was probably the first valid aircraft flight and——"

Tracy scowled at the academician. "I thought the American Wright brothers made the first heavier-than-air flights."

Stein chuckled. "Yes, and the Russians claimed it was a Ukrainian, I believe. The flights that the Wrights made in 1903 had a catapult-assisted takeoff. But Voisin's biplane took off under its own power and flew a one-kilometer circuit. But what I was getting at was that by 1918 the airplane was a modern reality, as a result of the necessities of war. Voisin himself built over ten thousand planes for the Allies. A year after the war, in 1919, the first aircraft were already flying the Atlantic.''

Tracy protested again. ''I thought it was Lindbergh in 1927 or so.''

''He made the first nonstop flight. They did it step by step in flying boats. Confound it, Tracy, stop interrupting. Look at the Second World War. Under its pressures were developed the first spaceship, the German V-two, nuclear fission, practical radar and a half dozen antibiotics in the field of medicine, among other things. Even during the so-called cold war an enormous number of discoveries were made by the militarists of various countries. In fact, the eruption into space was a development of the Cold War, in spite of flowery statements to the contrary. It was the competition between the United States and the Soviet Union which led first to the sputniks and finally to the first man on the moon.''

''However,'' Tracy said dryly, ''I have been in a few wars, and I'm just as glad that war has been eliminated.''

Betty frowned at him. She said, ''So are we, obviously, but father's point is that man's incentives for progress have been taken from him. We have eliminated war, but have found nothing to replace it.''

Tracy put butter and marmalade on another piece of

his toast. "All right," he said. "Tell me something about this International Congress of Guilds."

Stein said, "It's a planning body which coordinates all production, distribution——"

"You told me that the other day. Who composes it?"

"Representatives from all the different guilds. The Medical Guild, the Industrial Production Guild, the Communications Guild, the Transportation Guild, the——"

"All right. I get the message. Every useful type of work is represented in one guild or the other. How are these representatives appointed?"

The three of them looked at him as though the question was idiotic. Edmonds said, "Why they're elected by the membership of the guilds."

"I see," Tracy said, taking a sip of his coffee. "And this congress is the nearest thing to a government the world has these days."

"Yes."

Tracy tilted his head slightly as he looked at Jo Edmonds. He said, "You told me last night that the socioeconomic system today was anarchism. But what you're describing now isn't anarchy. Anarchy presupposes no government at all, which, of course, is nonsense in a highly industrialized society. What you're describing seems to be a highly refined type of syndicalism. I thought you were a student of socioeconomics."

Edmonds smiled wryly and said, "I was being facetious last night." He thought about it. "I don't believe that the present socioeconomic system fits any

222

of the cut-and-dried definitions of the past: capitalism, feudalism, socialism, communism. Perhaps you could make an argument for calling this a form of socialism. God knows, everybody who ever called himself a socialist had a different definition of what it was. In your day, some people accused Roosevelt of being a socialist. Hitler called himself a National Socialist. The British were supposedly under a socialist government, as were the Scandinavian countries, all of them complete with royal families, a holdover from feudalism. The Russians called themselves, interchangeably, both communist and socialist. Oh yes, the word socialist is elastic, so, if you wish, you could call this socialism.''

"Well, it sure as hell isn't capitalism," Tracy said, pouring more coffee.

Stein said, ''In point of fact, you didn't actually have classical capitalism in your own time, Tracy Cogswell. Practically all of the advanced nations had a system of what you might call State Capitalism.''

Tracy scowled at him. "How do you mean?"

"Where so-called free enterprise ended and government began was moot. High-ranking officials in both seemed interchangeable. A cabinet secretary, one day, would be president of a major corporation the next, or vice versa. Many of the larger corporations were subsidized in one way or the other. Oil and mining companies were allowed fabulously large tax deductions for depletion; billionaries such as Paul Getty sometimes paid no taxes at all. The subsidizing of shipping, both building ships and running shipping lines, was another example. If the socioeconomic system had been classical capitalism, it would have been a matter of sink or swim. If shipping couldn't compete with foreign lines, it would have gone under and the cheaper carriers of foreign countries would have been utilized. There are many other examples. Somewhat after the time you were, ah, put to sleep, Lockheed, one of the big airplane manufacturers, faced bankruptcy. The government loaned them hundreds of millions of dollars. Under classical capitalism, they would have been allowed to go under and more efficient competitors, such as Boeing, would have taken over that corporation's markets. No, I'm afraid that free enterprise in your time was a thing of the past. Even the farmers were subsidized, especially the very big ones.''

"Okay, okay," Tracy said impatiently. "As usual, we've gotten sidetracked. From what you say, this International Congress of Guilds is all you've got in the way of government. Now, how does somebody like you vote for a representative in it?" He looked at Walter Stein.

"Me?" the other said. "I'm not a member of a guild. The computers decided I wasn't needed by the Medical Guild. So I have no vote."

"Oh, great," Tracy said. "Nobody but members of a guild get to vote, and less than two percent of the population work, and hence, are members of guilds. Whatever happened to democracy?"

Jo Edmonds put down his napkin and said, "We seem to be defending a system that we're trying to eliminate, however . . ." He came to his feet and went into the living room and to the phone screen there. He dialed and then dialed again.

Finally, he came back and reseated himself and said to Tracy, "What was the last presidential election you experienced in America?"

Tracy scowled. "1956."

"That's what I thought. What was the population at that time?"

Tracy thought before saying, "Pushing two hundred million, as I recall."

"Yes, not quite but almost. Eisenhower won the election. He got thirty-five million votes. Between one out of five and one out of six of the population voted for him, in short. This is democracy? Once again, the term is somewhat elastic. Supposedly, Athens, during the Golden Age, achieved one of the greatest democracies of all time. But check back. Only male Athenian citizens were allowed the franchise. Slaves, and other noncitizens, who outnumbered the Athenians at least eight to one, were not allowed the vote. Neither were women. This is democracy?"

Tracy sighed. "Sidetracked again," he said. "Let's get down to the nitty-gritty. I want to know something about this underground of yours, your outfit for overthrowing things as they are and getting the human race back on the good old treadmill."

The three of them looked at each other with an almost apprehensive manner.

Tracy poured himself still more coffee and said impatiently, "How does your underground plan to overthrow the present system and what does it expect to take its place?'' He sighed again and added, ''I'm in, I suppose. After what I saw last night, I'd have to be in. I don't believe even you realize some of the ramifications of those programmed Dream Palaces.''

''How do you mean?'' Betty said.

''They've been developing for something like five years, Jo told me, so you've gotten used to the idea a step at a time. But they came on me like a slap in the face. The way things are now, you're only allowed eight hours at a time, of dreams, on the theory that for health's sake you've got to spend the other sixteen hours eating, exercising and getting some real sleep. Well, your wisenheimer computers have to figure out only one problem, getting real rest during the programmed dreaming. Then a dream addict could spend all his time at it.''

Jo said worriedly, ''But exercise and food——''

''Surely they could build something like an automatic massage machine to cover the exercise and the dreamers could be fed intravenously.''

''Good God,'' the academician blurted. ''You're right.''

''Yes,'' Tracy said, sipping away at the coffee. ''But we're off on a tangent again. What's your underground's program?''

There was a pause before the academician said, ''The fact is, we don't have one.''

Tracy stared at him unbelievingly. ''What do you mean? I want to know how you expect to get from here to there, and what it will look like when we reach it.''

''I know,'' the other nodded, ''but we don't have a

program. That's exactly why we brought you into this century, Tracy Cogswell. We want you to help us work out a plan of action and the new society of the future.''

''I'll be a sonofabitch,'' Tracy said. He put down his cup and stared around at the three of them, one by one. He rubbed a weary hand over his face before saying, ''Do I look like Thomas Jefferson, or Tom Paine, or Karl Marx, or whoever? I was a field man, not a theoretician. Sure, I've read a lot of the books, the classics of political economy, but I'm no scholar in the field. I followed orders and suggestions; I didn't think them up.''

''You know more about such things than any of the rest of us,'' Jo Edmonds said mildly.

''I doubt it. I'm not even very clear as yet on just how this system of yours works.''

Betty said, ''That's no problem, Tracy. We can give you several courses on the autoteacher to bring you up to date on details.''

He grunted in resignation and said, ''Let's get back to this underground organization, though why you call it an underground I don't know. From what you say it's perfectly legal to be above ground and in the open. It's international, I assume.''

''Well, yes,'' Stein nodded. ''Though, of course, we no longer have nations in the old sense. But Betty and I were born in North America, and Jo, here, in England.''

''How about the other members? Do they come from all parts of the world?''

''What other members?'' Betty said.

Chapter Fourteen

If she had thrown her coffee into his face, Tracy couldn't have been more taken aback. He said finally, "That can't possibly mean what I think it means."

The three of them looked embarrassed.

He pressed on. "Do you mean to tell me that you're the only members of this revolutionary underground organization you've been telling me about?"

Walter Stein said placatingly, and somewhat hurriedly, "There are a good many others who feel the same as we do, but without a program and a goal there is nothing about which to coalesce. Given a program, they would rally around and we could form a strong organization."

"Oh, good Jesus Christ," Tracy said in disgust. "You bring me across a century of time at the risk of my life and after ripping off twenty thousand dollars from me, to join an organization composed of three persons . . ."

"Four, now," Jo said mildly. "You declared yourself in."

". . . and without a program or any clear idea of what it wants."

Stein said, "We know what we want. We want to get the human race back on the road to progress. I repeat, it's turned to mush."

"Mush," Tracy said in disgust, and throwing his napkin to the table top as he came to his feet. "From what I saw last night, it's turning to gruel. I'm going in to study my Interlingua."

Betty looked up at him and said anxiously, "But how do you stand now?"

"I'm beginning to think I can stand anything," he said. "I don't know. Let me think about it. One of you come in later and help me out with getting that historic rundown on the past century. From now on, I'll spend half the day on Interlingua and the other half on trying to find out what has gone on, and what's going on."

He turned and left, not bothering to hide his feelings.

Tracy spent much of the next two weeks at the autoteacher, first perfecting his Interlingua then launching into his studies of what had transpired in the past ninety years since Academician Walter Stein had seized first his mind, then his physical body. He at first took a quick resume of this, accomplishing it in one day, then went back and picked out periods and subjects which particularly interested him and went into more detail. In some cases, he went into a great deal of detail. He didn't truly know what he was looking for, but he gathered a lot of information.

The autoteacher fascinated him. He realized that such a device was the only possible answer to the knowledge explosion. Utilizing it, a dedicated scholar of the old school could have become as universal a brain as a Roger Bacon, a Leonardo, or, say, a Benjamin Franklin . . . all updated.

The other three kept themselves continually available to answer his questions, though he could have done with the information in the Data Banks, usually. However, there was a certain advantage in personal conversation. You can't get into an argument with a data bank, no matter how sophisticated, and arguments sometimes bring out ideas.

They had become somewhat contrite in his presence now that they had revealed that their organization was nonexistent. They refrained from asking him if he had come up with anything in the way of answers to their problems, and he assumed that they figured that if he did he'd let them know . . . if there were any answers.

The brick wall he ran into was that it's hard to argue with success, and by all the criteria that had come down through the ages, the modern world was a success. Everybody had it made. Absolute abundance, absolute freedom to do any anything that the individual wanted to do. How can you talk a man into change when he has everything he wants? How can you approach the average man and say that the race is going to pot? Why should he give a damn? He had it made.

Back in Tracy's day, suppose you had approached a Henry Ford, a Howard Hughes, a Nelson Rockefeller, and said that as a result of the present politicoeconomic system the world was going to pot; pollution, population explosion, crime, narcotics, hunger in the backward countries, reoccurring war, depletion of natural resources, and on and on. Suppose that you had requested any of them to sponsor basic changes in the system. What would their response have been? They would have had you thrown out. They had it made. They didn't want any basic changes. Oh, yes, you might have gotten a contribution to help fight one or the other of the results of the overall system, say pollution . . . or, better still, crime . . . but you couldn't have convinced any of them about basic changes in the whole system. They had it made.

Most of his nights were spent with Betty and she made a perfect bed companion. He had never slept with a more frank woman, nor a more knowledgeable one. If nothing else, the present system of sex instructors certainly taught the students good technique. He doubted if there had ever been a period in history in which sex technique was more highly developed. It simply couldn't have been more developed.

It was about a week after the revelation of the three to him that Tracy surprised Betty. They were relaxed, after a particularly strenuous sexual encounter, and temporarily, at least, seated.

She said, making lazy talk, "Do you find life considerably better in this age, Tracy?"

"How do you mean?"

"Well," she said, "it must have been difficult, the life you led in your own time. Wars, prisons, poverty . . . I suppose that you spent the larger part of your life in want of one sort or the other. I assume you had your high points, success of one sort or the other. Perhaps a successful romance. You still had romantic love in your day, didn't you?''

He looked from his pillow to hers. "In my day? Are you suggesting that you don't have it now?''

"Oh, don't be silly, darling.''

''Well, what in the devil is the relationship between you and me? I was considering asking you to marry me, if other things work out.''

''Marry you?'' she said in wonder. "Good heavens, how anachronistic can you get? We don't have marriage anymore, Tracy. The institution of marriage was largely a property relationship, a legal contract. The laws that regulated it were devised when private property came in and primitive institutions were overthrown. A man wanted to be sure that his own children, particularly his sons, inherited his property. To accomplish this, he had to be sure that his woman—his wife—slept with nobody but him. It got quite extreme sometimes. The way the Greeks kept their wives cooped up in their homes, even when the men were out spending the evening with pretty boys. The ultimate extreme was the harem of Asia and Africa. They were attempting to frustrate the old adage that a child knows its mother but it's a wise one that knows its father.''

Tracy said stiffly, ''The same situation didn't apply in the West of my day, particularly in America. We married for love.''

''Did you truly?'' she said, with mockery in her voice. ''All of you? Or was it a society in which women were second-class citizens, dependent on the men they married and hence desperate to make 'a good marriage?' Did a man who might be as ugly as a monkey and with a nasty temper and a tendency to cheat on his wife at every opportunity, but who also had a million dollars or so in his bank account, have any difficulty taking his pick of the girls? And didn't he demand that she be a virgin, though he had been having all the sex he wanted for years?''

Tracy scowled and said, ''Okay. So how does it differ now?''

''We no longer have property. A woman is no longer dependent on a man, nor are his children. She doesn't have to worry about them. There is no longer any need for marriage. The only reason for a woman sleeping with a man is that she likes him and wants to. There is no marriage and no divorce.''

He said stiffly, ''Weren't your father and mother married?''

''Certainly not. And I hardly know her. She didn't like children. I don't know why she ever bothered to have me. And she doesn't particularly like my father anymore. Currently, I think she's up in the Alps. She likes to ski and has no interest whatsoever in social questions.''

Tracy said, ''But you live with your father. That's a family relationship.''

She shrugged that off. ''We live together because we like each other. Father likes children and consequently raised me, rather than turning me over to the Children Guild, as most children usually are. And I like him. I don't always live with him. From time to time I've met a man, or for some other reason have taken off for periods of as long as a year or more. But largely we find ourselves compatible and live together.''

Tracy shook his head. He had always considered himself in advance of the mores of his time, but this was far beyond him.

She said, "But you didn't answer my question. Do you find life considerably better in this age?"

He thought about it for a moment before saying bluntly, "No. I dislike it."

She couldn't disguise her astonishment, and said, "You *do?* But why? Aside, of course, from the task we've set ourselves. Materially——"

He interrupted her, and said slowly, "A few days ago your father used as an example a man of the year 1855, before the American Civil War. Suppose you had taken him forward in time to my era, circa 1955. Would he have truly liked it, after the immediate surprises, after he had adapted a bit? I doubt it. I doubt if he would have liked the people, after the brash honesty of the American of the frontier years. I doubt if he could have stomached the relationship between the sexes. The new freedom. Women's clothing would have shocked him. The fact that they participated in politics, had the vote, worked shoulder to shoulder with men in factories, or wherever, would all have cut across the grain. He would have been contemptuous of the food, with the TV dinners, the packaged and canned meals, as compared to his former meat and potato diet. In his day, men drank to get smashed, and usually wound up in a sight, passed out, or in jail. In my time, drinking was all but universal, among both men and women, and cocktails and other mixed drinks were usual, instead of the three fingers of red eye, straight booze, as consumed in his time. Sure, he would have been amazed by cars and airplanes, and the speed at which they traveled, but he probably would have preferred the more comfortable, easygoingness of a horse and buggy. He would have been contemptuous of the fact that homosexuality was winked at, if not openly condoned. In his era they probably would have lynched a queer. Oh, he wouldn't have been at all happy in my time."

"And that's how you feel about the present?" She was frowning slightly, his point of view not exactly coming through to her.

"More or less," he said. "I just can't adapt, and don't particularly want to. Perhaps I'm too old. Too set in my attitudes. If I was a teenager, it might be different."

Betty said, "But, what, for instance? You have everything now."

He smiled grimly. "Perhaps it's like your father said. Perhaps I don't want everything I want." He tried to work it out. "Take an example. This might sound picayune, but it's just one thing out of scores. Throwing away clothes, each night, after just one day of wear. I know, you explained that less labor is involved in the long run than if you laundered them or dry cleaned them. But I was born in a working class family and often we were up against it. It's just completely against the grain, throwing away perfectly good clothing. I know, I know, it's recycled; but I know it intellectually but reject it inwardly."

"What else?" she said and there was mystification in her voice.

"Oh, possibly stupid little things. For instance, the other night you dialed a dish at dinner that would have cost a good many dollars in my time. You took one look at it and changed your mind, and dumped it, and ordered something else. When I was a kid we were taught to eat everything on our plate. Hell, we didn't have to be taught; we either did or we went hungry."

"What else?" she said.

He drug air into his lungs. "Nobody works. I believe that everybody should work. Everybody should do something . . . besides playing with a piece of jade, like Jo does, or the equivalent."

She said, a bit of indignation in her voice, "As you know, I have similar beliefs to your own on that score, and so do father and Jo."

"Yes, but you and your father and Jo are a rather small minority," he said unhappily. "But to go on. Your sexual mores upset me as much as that man from 1855 would be upset in 1955. I just can't accept your complete permissiveness, your rejection of what we used to call love, the disappearance of marriage, your acceptance of group sex. The other day you told me that Jo was perfectly normal, he liked girls and men both, or group sex for that matter. Well, for me that isn't exactly normal, and inwardly I revolt against it."

"And what else?"

He tried to think of some of the other things, and said finally, "I don't want to seem like a prude but your attitude toward narcotics is unacceptable to me. Above

all is this new code that anything is premissable between consenting adults, even things like sadism, up to
and including gladiator fights. I just can't get the feeling of allowing anything to go, anything at all. Bull
fighting, pit dog fights, bear baiting, cock fights. In my
day, such things weren't allowed. And, as far as I'm
concerned, they still shouldn't be allowed. I was of the
opinion that man had arisen above such things."

"You don't have to attend them," she said reasonably. "And you don't have to take narcotics or have
group sex. All these things are left up to the individual.
Why should you care what the next person does?"

"I know, I know," he said. "I didn't expect it to
make sense to you, any more than that guy from before
the Civil War would have made sense to me. But that's
not all. Perhaps the big thing I miss is the companion-
ship of my own day. You see, I spent most of my life in
the company of such men as Dan Whiteley. We were
caught up in the movement, the ideal of building a
better world. We sacrificed. Sometimes we all but
starved together. Sometimes some of those closest
friends died for the cause. In my time, I have been there
when one or the other of them were cut down . . .
sometimes when attempting to protect my life."

Betty said softly, "I'm sorry, Tracy, darling. What
you say doesn't make too much sense to me, but I can
see you are unhappy in this world of ours."

"It's not your fault," Tracy said. "It's nobody's
fault. It's just that I'm a fish out of water. There is no
reality for me in this world. You've all been kind to me
. . . especially you, Betty."

After a time she said, "Tracy, do you love me? I mean in the old sense of the word. What you meant in your day."

He said, "Yes, I love you, Betty."

She said softly, "Nobody ever said that to me before."

Chapter Fifteen

It was a few days later, when Tracy had left his desk for lunch, that he brought up the question of space. Only Jo Edmonds was in the dining room; both Betty and her father had gone into town on some errand or other. If you could call it going into town. It was one of the things most difficult for Tracy to accept in this age. There were no stores, no restaurants, in view of the fact that you could order any prepared food you wished in the privacy of your own home, no governmental buildings, no gasoline stations. What was left of the old town of Tangier spread all up and down the coast and consisted of widely spaced villas strategically located to take full advantage of the marvelous view out over the straits.

Jo said, in the way of greeting, "How go the studies?"

Tracy went over to the autobar and dialed himself an aperitif before sitting down.

"I've gotten to the space program," he said. "It's rather interesting. I understand that now it's almost completely abandoned. What would you say was the climax of the whole project?''

Jo had been dialing his lunch. He considered the question. ''I should think the Russians landing four men on Mars, some decades ago.''

''I haven't gotten to that, as yet,'' Tracy said. ''What did they find?''

''More or less what everybody expected them to find, I should think. Nothing. Oh, they picked up material of interest to the scientist blokes, I suppose, but there wasn't anything really startling. It rather gave the kiss of death to the space program. Practically everybody lost whatever interest remained.''

Tracy dialed his own meal, including a half bottle of claret. One thing he had to concede to this age. It was impossible to get a second-rate drink, or a less than superlative dish. They simply didn't make them.

He said, ''One of you mentioned, the other day, a manned Jupiter probe.''

''That's right,'' the other said. ''It was going to have to be a one-man affair, in view of the limited space available for fuel, food and air on such a long jaunt.''

Tracy said, ''But after they built the ship, nobody would go?''

''That's right,'' Jo laughed. ''I don't blame them. I sure as hell wouldn't.''

''Why not just send an unmanned, automatic ship?''

''Oh, they had already done that,'' Edmonds said. ''But there are limits to what an unmanned spaceship can do, don't you know? Particularly at that distance. There was some discussion at the time of the possibility

240

that some of the larger satellites of Jupiter, Ganymede, in particular, might be able to sustain life. It's got a diameter of some 3,000 miles, which makes it half again as large as our Luna. The scientists seem to think that none of the other planets, Mercury, Venus, Mars, and so forth could support life, but Ganymede just might.''

"Interesting," Tracy said.

"I suppose so. I went through a period as a youngster when I was all gung-ho about space. But there's little to do about it now.''

Their food had come and they were both eating.

Tracy said curiously, "What ever happened to the spaceship they built for the Jupiter trip.''

The other frowned. "It seems to me they put it in mothballs. Isn't that the term you used to use?''

"Yes. You mean it's still there?''

"I suppose so," Jo said. "It was about twenty years ago when they wrapped the space program up. Oh, they still have the artificial communications satellites and the observatories on the moon, also automated; but there's no more original research going on, at least so far as I know.''

Tracy nodded. "More of the indications that the race is turning to mush, eh?''

"I suppose so.''

Tracy asked, "Where's the nearest Dream Palace, Jo?''

The other was surprised at the question. "Why, right here in Tangier.''

"Where?''

Jo looked at him, frowning slightly. "It's located in the former palace of the sultans on the Kasbah. It's one of the few buildings that's come down from the old days. In a minor sort of way, the Kasbah is now a Pleasure Center. Most people go over to Gibraltar, up to Torremolinos, or down to Rabat for their, ah, sinning. But the Kasbah has a few places, including a very popular duo of nightclubs for homosexuals. One for men, one for lesbians. Rooms on the second floor, of course."

Tracy said, "I think I'll go on over. Will you check me out again on how to get a programmed dream?"

Jo was obviously disappointed but he said, "Well, yes, of course."

Tracy said, "I'll be gone for the full eight hours."

Jo Edmonds said, "It's your affair. When I took you to the Dream Palace in Torremolinos and you asked me if I had ever tried it and asked me what, I told you that it wasn't any of your business. And you went into the gardens of Hasan something or other."

"Yes."

"Well, have you ever read the poem of Samuel Coleridge, *Kubla Khan?* It goes like this:

    In Xanadu did Kubla Khan
    A stately pleasure-dome decree:
    Where Alph, the sacred river, ran
    Through caverns measureless to man
    Down to a sunless sea.
    So twice five miles of fertile ground
    With walls and towers were girdled round."

"Yes," Tracy said. "I had a lot of time to read, in

242

hospitals, concentration camps . . . prisons. Yes, I've read it. I understand that he wrote it under the influence of laudanum, didn't recognize it when he came out of the influence of the drug, and never finished it.''

"So I've read too," Jo said. "However, I can recommend Xanadu. I suspect, even more worthwhile than your Hasan whatever-his-name gardens.''

"No thanks," Tracy told him. "I have another thing in mind." He allowed himself a grin at the other. "Something more exciting.''

"I doubt it," Jo said, in resignation. He hadn't expected Tracy Cogswell to get hooked on the programmed dream bit.

But Tracy Cogswell not only spent eight hours at the Dream Palace that day but every day for the next two weeks or more. His way of life became somewhat frenetic. He allowed himself six hours of sleep, exercises hard, usually jogging and shadow punching, for two hours, and spent the balance of his time at hurried meals and before his autoteacher. The other three saw precious little of him; even Betty, who still occupied his bed.

Needless to say, they were distressed at his actions. Finally, at dinner one night, Walter Stein confronted him on the matter.

"Tracy," he said, his voice conciliatory, "I believe that Jo has already told you that it is quite possible to become so addicted to the programmed dreams that there is no return. Your real life goes down the drain.''

"It won't happen to me," Tracy told him.

Jo said, "That's what they all say, some of them

243

even after they've been hooked. Some get hooked on women and other sensuous pleasures, some on the thrills of war, various things. What have you been specializing in, Tracy?''

Tracy smiled at him. He said, ''I've been piloting that spaceship the Russians flew to Mars. I started with blast-off, and now, each day, I've been taking up where I left off at the previous eight-hour period. I've finally made the whole round trip, including the stay on Mars.''

''Good heavens,'' Betty blurted. ''Why?''

Tracy didn't answer her. Instead, he looked at Stein and said, ''Would it be possible to take that Jupiter probe out of mothballs?''

The academician was flustered. ''Why . . . why I suppose so. All the pertinent information would be in the computer data banks. And there are still some technicians, those in charge of the automated communications satellites and the moon observatories. From time to time it is necessary to launch a new satellite, or send equipment to Luna. If there were any repairs, or whatever, undoubtedly they could be made.''

Tracy took a sip of his wine before saying, ''If I volunteered to pilot that Jupiter probe, would it attract much attention?''

Walter Stein frowned. ''Probably,'' he said. ''People are jaded now. Any new fad, any new excitement, will bring their attention. There's precious little in the news, year in and year out, to cause excitement. A while ago someone invented a new game, Battle Chess.

Within six months, half the population of Earth was playing it, with world champions and everything else. A year later, it was forgotten. Yes, you'd attract a great deal of attention. On your way out, they'd be on the edge of their chairs, waiting for you to have a failure of your spacecraft. When and if you returned, they'd probably forget your name within months.''

Jo said mildly, ''You don't impress me as being the glory-grabber type, old chap.''

Tracy looked at him. He said, ''While going to the Dream Palace eight hours of each day, I was also studying on the autoteacher everything I could about space and the training of an astronaut, or cosmonaut. I'm a man of action. This life I've been leading with you three isn't for me. I want to be up and doing something.''

They were aghast. Stein blurted, ''But the program, the new goal, the new society to plan?''

Tracy shook his head at them wearily. He said, ''I worked it over and over. There is no program of change. The fact is, there's nothing particularly wrong with this socioeconomic system. It works as well, or better, than any in history.'' He took a deep breath before going on. ''The shortcoming is in the people who live in it.''

Betty said indignantly, ''But, Tracy, they're destroying themselves, and, as a result, eventually the race!''

''It's not the fault of the system,'' he insisted. ''It's the fault of the individuals. Everybody doesn't destroy themselves under it. You three for instance. And that

245

small percentage you say are still needed by the International Congress of Guilds to keep things going.''

Walter Stein sighed. "I suspect that you're right," he said. "Frankly, I never have been able to vizualize a social system to replace this one, even if the people would stand for it and they probably wouldn't."

Tracy said, "Where is the Jupiter probe located?"

"In North America, at the spaceport near what used to be the city of Greater Washington."

"Will you help me make arrangements to volunteer to pilot it to Jupiter?"

Walter Stein said lowly, and in resignation, "Yes, certainly. I brought you here, against your will. You have always been free to go. My big dream has turned out to be a mistake, but that is not your fault. You tried. You did your best."

The takeoff was less than two months later.

Tracy Cogswell had made his goodbyes to Betty and Academician Walter Stein, and to Jo Edmonds, whom he had grown to like increasingly over the months. The three of them had accompanied him to the Greater Washington area and were present at the blast-off.

Three persons out of four in the world were glued to their tri-di sets. It went like clockwork. The spacecraft was in perfect condition.

Even with the new nuclear engines, the trip was a long one. Each day Tracy made a laser-beam report back to Earth.

Each day, at that time, the Steins and Jo Edmonds sat before their screens, waiting for him. Sometimes he would send them a personal message, usually a humorous quip . . . which was understandable. Precious little was happening that was new, nor would it, until he reached the vicinity of the giant planet.

And as he did, at long last, Earth's interest in him grew to new heights. Would he make it? Would Jupiter grab him in her powerful gravity and suck him down into the swirling gases that seemed to cover her surface?

He was within a couple of thousand kilometers of Ganymede when the tragedy struck.

He had been making more reports than usual as Jupiter grew larger before him. So he was on the laser beam when it happened.

Suddenly, in the midst of a description of the satellite Ganymede, he blurted, "Something has just materialized only a few kilometers from me. It's a giant . . . a giant spaceship . . . It must be as big as an aircraft carrier, like the *Forrestal* . . . it's gigantic!"

His voice was high, almost shrill. "There's something strange about it. I can feel thought waves or something coming from it . . . they're malevolent. It's like a wave of hate . . . I . . . . I can feel it! It's monstrous! They hate us! They hate the idea of there being another intelligent life form in the galaxy. They hate us! Hate us!"

He broke off for a moment, as though overwhelmed, and then took it up again, his voice still rising. "Something is happening . . . . I'm being drawn toward it. . . . Some sort of magnetic tractor force is pulling me in."

His last words were shouted. "Earth! EARTH! . . . DEFEND! DEFEND! . . .

And those were the last words Tracy Cogswell ever spoke.

Within twenty-four hours, Earth was shifting into high gear, and within forty-eight the rioting mobs were burning the Pleasure Centers.

AFTERWARD

The next few weeks were hectic. Half the world was taking intensified courses in subjects involving space. The International Congress of Guilds was organizing a crash program to revive the space projects of yesteryear. The Steins and Jo Edmonds split up, with Jo returning to England and Betty going out to the American west coast to apply for a position at one of the new spaceports. It wasn't as yet completed and wouldn't be for approximately a month, so she returned east to stay with her father.

On their first night together they sat and watched the news of the tri-di. Almost all of it was devoted to the new crash program to get man back into space. Betty said lowly, "I wonder whatever happened to Tracy."

Her father looked at her in surprise. "You mean you don't understand?"

"Understand what?"

"Betty, don't you see? There was nothing out there. Perhaps, one day, man will find other intelligent life in the stars, but this wasn't it. This was Tracy's plan to unite the race, to put it back on the road to progress and expansion. The expansion into space is beginning with a fury. Perhaps, for a time, a century or so, it will largely be with defense in mind. But then, after we have progressed far, far beyond the point we are at now, the truth will undoubtedly come home to us and though we will continue our march toward our destiny, the stars, it will no longer be with military matters in mind. I suspect that Tracy Cogswell has taken care of that.''

''Taken care of it? But where is Tracy?''

Her father shook his head sadly. ''Dead by now, I assume. Surely his supplies have failed by now. I suspect that he is in orbit about Jupiter, that he has become in his ship, one of Jupiter's satellites. One day, an Earth military space cruiser, or a group of them, will probably cautiously reconnoiter the area. They will find his dead ship and that will be the tipoff. He will probably have left a note of explanation, or a tape, to explain the whole farce. Then we will realize what a hero he was. That he made a false scare report to spur on the race and in so doing made a martyr of himself.''